the one about the icebergs

AND OTHER STORIES

RUSSELL CRAIG RICHARDSON

Station Hill Press
BARRYTOWN, NY

Published by Station Hill Press, the publishing project of the Institute for Publishing Arts, Inc., 120 Station Hill Road, Barrytown, NY 12507, New York, a not-for-profit, tax-exempt organization [501(c)(3)].

Online catalogue: www.stationhill.org
email: publishers@stationhill.org

Cover and interior Design: Sherry Williams

Library of Congress Cataloging-in-Publication Data available
ISBN: 9781581772449
ISBN epub: 9781581772456

Manufactured in the United States

Land Acknowledgment
In the spirit of truth and equity, it is with gratitude and humility that we acknowledge that the Institute for Publishing Arts, Inc. and Station Hill Press reside on the sacred homelands of the Munsee and Muhheaconneok people, who are the original stewards of this land. Today, due to forced removal, the community resides in Northeast Wisconsin and is known as the Stockbridge-Munsee Community.

for Dorota

Contents

the one about kobi

THE CITY is a language held together by stories: Novels stretch north-south; poems bind east-west; History and Science zigzag from basement to rooftop. Each neighborhood threaded with library shelves, shifting like the rivers, like the clouds, like the birds, like their flocks. Like us.

The whole skyline slathered in images, crawling over its skin, in the sky, in the spaces between, sheathes, mirrors, wishes and prompts. Only seen intermittently, with the right mood, the right password, the right handshake, the right pair of eyes.

Tunnels all look the same in the dark. There's a lot of places down there, a lot of objects and sharp edges, and a cross-section curiously reveals that the levels of the subway system and the contours of the street system do not necessarily coincide. Some elevated tracks in one part of town correspond to deep canyons in another part; other sections of long, downward slope will suddenly expose you out in mid-air, because the streets have been falling more precipitately still; or you realize you must now be burrowing underwater, crossing under the river. It's a mistake to think of the land as flat, and the tracks laid out neatly beneath. And the shafts and cross-tunnels do more of the same.

And the sewers under that. And then the inevitable apocryphal burial grounds; and then the groaning bedrock. Then the magma. On to the center of the Earth.

A lot of people could live down there, or get around, and a lot of people do. Other creatures, too.

I first ran into Kobi just over a year ago, in the first days of autumn, and he let slip almost immediately that he wasn't human, but something else that had escaped into human form. Well, I thought, why not? everybody needs their narrative, who am I to sink this guy's boats? I'd probably seen him around before, out of the corner of my eye, as I scuttled under the city to some irrelevant rendezvous or went about what my brother dismissively called my 'business', but I first engaged with Kobi last October. He was shuffling along one of the underpasses that make up the inside/outside warren that is the Port Authority under Forty-second St. in New York City. It's a carefully subdivided labyrinth of false inclusions and exclusions that canalizes people without the need for signage or barrier. If you need to get *there*, you have to go down *here*; if you can't afford a ticket, then you have to go up *this* staircase and down *that* corridor, walk against the flow of pedestrians, and double back through the exit gate, which is usually, often, sometimes, left ajar. You will then find yourself at the end of a warmer platform, or most likely shuffling in the complexly indented trace of a bowel which is nevertheless a topographic circle. Shuffling and muttering. Clasping a proudly printed recyclable shopping bag to your chest.

Though shambolic and hunched, Kobi did not give out an air of menace, at least not to me, he seemed oddly familiar, there was something endearing in his movements, like some oversized child or tame bear. Something to do with the lumbering slowness of his gait. As if you could never be in any danger because of his lack of speed. Apparent lack of speed. And then, a sign from one animal to another, that curious and irregular wheezing, the prey forever halt to catch its breath, which the predator, myself in atavistic mode, notices: the weakness, heightened, and accordingly paused. And the voice, as of an old bluesman half-singing, half-musing to himself, a shadow. A harmless black guy, ancient aimless odoriferous in the fug of the subway.

How not at all.

This day now, the first chill of approaching winter, an edge on the outside air, up top, I remember now as I leapt from train to train, why was I taking the train? I could have should have walked the whole way, but that nip in the air, it forced me underground, as Kobi had skipped sideways, dodging the considerable draughts, briskly between trains, I sensed this shape murmuring, pausing every few paces to rest his forearm on the tiled wall of the corridor. Incongruency of the advertising hoardings. I came upon him at the very moment he began fumbling in his shopping bag. He let drop an object which rolled slowly into my path: a matt black sphere that fell with a dull thud and slowly rolled towards me. I stooped and picked it up, then handed it back to him, black. Those eyes. He looked up at me, as if with familiarity, breathed in that shallow way a couple of times then gave out the most eloquent grunt I have ever heard. It at once acknowledged his own clumsiness, then that 'this'—what I could observe of his external appearance – was not his natural state; along with a gratitude that I had intervened, the corridor sloping awkwardly away down to the next interchange, a little gratitude for that, not too much, all wrapped in a glimpse of what would have happened had I not been there at that moment, at that place, forced to stop by my awareness that here was a being that could be overpowered, or had I simply stepped over the rolling ball and carried on my hurried way. And why hurried? Then he held out a crabbed hand, I placed the squash ball in his upturned palm. The spider web of darker lines lacing the rubber, gauging its heft, then back into a pocket of his overcoat. An old-fashioned heavy tweed overcoat, like everyone used to wear in the middle of the last century, in the very first color photographs. I've seen some of them. Kobi waved me on with a gesture that managed an elegance rather than a curt dismissal, as if to say, 'Well, here we are. I am I, and Thou art Thee.' And that was the first time, our zero moment.

Living with my mother and my brother was getting hard. Firstly, because the place was too small, and then, my brother was almost never home. He had his things, and he had his friends and associates, whoever they were. He'd go off for days at a time, then turn up at four in the morning. I'd wake up right before the sound of the key sliding into the lock, as if time were running ahead of itself, or my ears never slept. Then wait for his stolid, heavy footsteps on the walk-up. More often than not, he'd tread on me on the way to the bathroom, or if I'd managed to squirrel my way under the table, where I could stretch out a bit, he might stumble over my feet and curse me, kick out at me. I could tell by my mother's breathing that she was playing possum, trying to avoid confrontation. Other times my brother would be calm, and open the window to sit on the fire escape and smoke. Once or twice, I crawled out and sidled alongside. He didn't want me to smoke whatever it was he was smoking. He'd hold the cigarette out of my reach and tut-tut, uh-unh, not for you. Like I said, no respect. Sibling hierarchy and all that. I'd sit in my underwear and watch the dawn with him. "Put some clothes on," he'd say, "You'll freeze your nuts off." Then, he'd thump me on the shoulder. Good Times, you might say. And in the morning, he'd vacuum up the contents of my mother's fridge and be gone. And we'd wonder if each when might be the last.

The second time I ran into Kobi, it was as though he was waiting for me, at the end of a platform, sitting on a bench alone, hunched over his bag, eyes closed nodding to an unseen beat. I was upon him before I realized who it was, and I could tell he was clocking my sneakers. He held up his hand in a benediction, or like some orchestra conductor. It was near Midwinter, and bitter cold outside. It had snowed the week before: real snow, you understand, not fake christmas decoration; and the gray ruts in the half-melted, refrozen ice made walking all but impossible. There was no-one on the street anymore and the subway cops weren't bothering to move the old guys on, as long as they didn't interfere with the other passengers. At least that's what I assumed. I had heard they'd steam in every morning and scoop everyone up, none too friendly, dump them all in Jersey, and let them find their own way back, or not, as the case might be. Garden State graves. The lost and the lonely. But it was Kobi. He motioned me to sit down, and I sat, more or less next to him, which I suppose is about as close as anyone had come for a good while. He rummaged in his sack and took out a tin of peaches. Deftly, he used one of those cruel looking old-fashioned openers, the ones with a triangular point at one end and a bottle opener at the other, and pierced a few holes in the top, before swilling down the syrup. Once he'd done that, he took a bit more care to peel the rest of the lid halfway, pulling it back with his fingers, and grabbed some slivers of peach. He caught me looking at him. Held out the tin. "Good stuff: Florida." When it became clear I wasn't going to take him up on his offer, he shrugged and went back to extracting the pieces of fruit. "Gotta keep your core temperature up." He stuck his finger almost in my face, "I know what you're thinking," he said. I must've looked blank. A little guilty, perhaps, but blank. I'm pretty sure I was unreadable.

I looked at the last sliver of peach as he slid it into his mouth. The train came.

And then he said something I wish he hadn't. As I stood up and waited for the doors to open, he fixed my eye and said, "I'm sorry about your brother. It's not fair"

I got on the train. I saw Kobi getting laboriously to his feet and limping off, as if he'd been waiting for me, and now he could go. Go where? Where was home? He was right about us meeting again, though. But he was wrong about my brother. When I got home, he was crashed out on the couch, his cigarette still glued to his lip. I carefully pried it away, took it, and quietly, silently, slid open the window. Once on the fire escape, I inspected the cigarette, lit up and took a drag. It didn't seem anything special. A second hit, letting the smoke fold itself out of my mouth and hang in the still, frigid air, frost on everything. A half-moon picking out the ice as if it were mica, mica snow, mica stars, my mica fingernails, mica eyelids. Every movement of my head, or my hands, or the languid world, left trails of mica flakes, glistening, mica comets coming for us all. I clipped the cigarette, crawled back inside, and put it on the rim of the ashtray, the smoke hanging impossibly static in the window frame. I lay under the table and stared back at myself sitting outside the window staring up at the mica stars running backwards through my brother's smoke. No panics tonight.

This winter wasn't shaping up well. I don't mind the cold, but I had plans, places to go, people to meet, needed time to move out of my mother's place, or get her out from under my feet, and keep myself from under hers. Impossibly sad to see her stupidly worrying about me. I can worry stupidly enough for the both of us. But, naturally, I wasn't actually worried about me at all. Because at that time, I was only looking in one direction, if at all. Who knows where the train would be coming from? I mean, it could fall on my head from above, or burst up out of the ground. Through the windows or through the front door. I needed my own place. At least a lock-up, a lock-in, where I could hide away if I needed to. Maybe I was looking both ways a little even then, without being aware of it.

The next days were a mess, I had tiny scalpels scraping under my fingernails all the time, and zigzag lines in the corners of my vision, like a migraine, minus the headache. Sometimes. Small mercies. The cold was really biting the way it can only be in a big city, the clouds down to the tops of the buildings. The wind putting everyone's life in turmoil at every cross street. If it would snow again, at least the beauty would redeem that bittercold a little. But no: designers had been toiling to pattern weather that made mockery of human ingenuity, and hubris in daring to even think of inventing clothes. Better we should stand naked in rags on mound and promontory, lips shading blue in the inclemency. I scuttled around the subterranean world, dodging any exposure to the elements, I suppose I was looking for Kobi, niggled by his ill-starred comment. What was that? He didn't even know I had a brother, not then, not till much later. I'm glad I kept mental notes. The dates don't match, but he said what he said, and I heard what I heard. A conundrum.

The ridiculousness of the situation struck me. How was I supposed to find one old guy again in the underbelly of a city of twenty-five million people, be they real or imaginary? At that time, I didn't even know his name, nor have the slightest idea of where he lived, I mean by that where he slept at night, if he did sleep at night. He wasn't one of those guys who pushes half a house around with him in a shopping cart, he only had his clothes, mainly his tweed coat. He had no friends down there, or anywhere else, and I certainly didn't know anyone who hung out in the tunnels. I suppose I'd designated him as a tunnel dweller in some sense, I'd never seen him outside the system, and he did lurk awfully close to the platform ends with 'Authorized Personnel Only' and Kobi didn't look like 'Authorized Personnel' to me, much. And how would he have found me, ever? Even the casual routes I took around the city spread out to cover miles and miles, levels and layers. I never liked to repeat a journey exactly, something I'd learnt from my brother. Always vary this twist, or that turn, get to the same place always by a different path, make it hard for anyone who was watching or tracking you. That's the way to do it, in my opinion, start behaving like that as a kid, as a game, take it so far into your past, and into your way of being, that no-one can predict what you will do in any situation. Make it first nature, never mind second nature. Oh, my brother, he had his tracts and rants. I used to tell him he was too suspicious, and he would rabbit punch me, and tell me I wasn't suspicious enough, that they were already watching me, and slowly, I'd start crossing streets for no reason, sprinting down alleyways, pausing outside doorways for a half a minute before entering. Just a game, you understand. Walk one way, but really be paying attention to the other sidewalk, in the other direction, and come to think of it, that's how I'd first sidled up to Kobi, out of the corner of his eye and mine. Kobi, it turned out, could do the same thing, but without moving. Like some old detectives or assassins could follow their targets from in front, always in the wrong place to be seen.

On this day, obviously, he was somewhere else, or so carefully wrapped up in his own routes that we were not going to intersect, or he was avoiding me by standing behind pillars or moving against the flow of passengers, sitting when they stood and moving left when I, school of fishes; they, murmuration of starlings, swerved right. Anyway, I didn't find him, and my fingers were still tingling from the cold. I sat up at street level in a cheap diner on Ninth, staring out at the weather channel, warming up my hands, trying to stop the nails being blue and the quicks crisp and bloodied. Woolen gloves don't work: they get wet, they freeze up, their ice needles dig into your fingertips and you're lost, surrendered to comfort only to beckon the enemy treacherous within. My own wardrobe was pretty simple: lots of layers in winter and not so many in the summer. The only truly outrageous accessories I owned were invisible to most people. My contact lenses, which again, had been presented to me by my brother: everybody wears lenses these days, unless you're one of those ostentatious types who insists on wearing spectacles, or goggles, even. But mine are special, even by the standards of Metropolitan Society and high-end gamers. Simply put, a good pair of contacts could set you back the best part of a year's salary, assuming you had a job, or make quite a dent in your inheritance, if you were one of the young-and-fancy-free beautiful people. Mine were evidently something quite special: no markings no logo; light and flexible yet somehow robust; and a perfect adaptive fit to my eyes—you'd never know I was wearing them. What's more, they seemed to be permanently on, and connected to—as far as I could make out—every running network. I don't know who was taking care of the bills. Obviously, my brother had obtained them by means other than his job: a) he never had a job; b) his trust fund, (our mother still worked all available hours to pay our rent); or c) his enterprise and successes on the stock market, (he was, basically, a thief). But optical devices as fancy as these could hardly be stolen, family ties or not, and there is no way he would have slipped them to me without some fuss. Unless he didn't know what he had stolen. That seemed scarily unlikely. They were just very good. And no-one could tell I had them in, or so I thought.

It was more than a week after my fruitless and I will now admit somewhat paranoid and careless attempt to find Kobi again. Now he had found me, I have to see it that way, because he slid in out of nowhere, and was suddenly just there—right where I was about to step. He was sitting on a bench, an uncomfortable structure designed by an architect, or the evil and abject minion of an architect, to resemble a bench or a seat, but to feel like a bicycle crossbar, or a rough-hewn log. Not a place to sit comfortably, and in no way a place where a person, a human person, could contort their human body into any shape and retain a purchase, or the possibility of sleep. A train pulled in, the crowd swelled, the crowd thinned and parted, and lo and behold, there sat Kobi staring calmly up at me. He scanned my face, then looked intently at my eyes. The train pulled away. In the lee of the eventual silence after, "That's a lot of hardware you got there." They weren't even turned on. Invisible. He looked closer, and I swear his manner was more that of a doctor, or an ophthalmologist, not some bum in the subway. Kobi moved his head back and forth, peering at my eyes, then pressing my temples gently, but firmly, tilted my head to-and-fro until he was satisfied.

"Grafted?" he asked. I shook my head, a shudder, more like, I couldn't bear the idea of eye surgery. I'm sensitive like that.

"No. Welded."

"Glued, you mean."

Everything is temporary, everything flows, thankfully.

"It's gonna hurt like hell when you take 'em out."

I confessed I wasn't planning on taking them out any time soon.

"You'd better, or you'll get the worms."

Which is how I learned I was wearing some highly unusual kit—something Kobi was intimately familiar with, to boot.

My brother was at home. My mother was cooking, something I hadn't known her do unprompted for months. There was no reason, it would have looked like a normal family evening to any outside observer. But this was the first time we'd all accidentally been calm in the same space together for at least a season. It had been hot, hot that last time. Not so today. I sat on a corner of the sofa and looked across the rooftops, between the buildings at the skyline. Too cold to go out onto the roof itself and look down on the other roofs or look down onto those as those above us looked down onto us. The order of things. That day, the hot, hot day, I'd been in my shorts and vest, dangling my legs over the edge. My brother had been speaking at me for some time, apparently, but I hadn't tuned in. He did that thing where someone grabs you by the shoulders, if you're sitting on a rooftop or a bridge, and makes as if to push you off, but they've really got you pretty tight before they shake you. I didn't like it though. My brother just laughed at my ranting and raving. He said, "You were miles away. I thought you were going to float away like a feather off a pigeon's tail." And he did a little mime gesture of figures-of-eight falling, falling. I was miles away, in my own private gravity, falling, falling. Or infinity symbols. "Thinking," I said.

"Thinking? Oh, I get it: Serious Stuff..." He kneaded his wispy chin in an annoying way. "I wonder what that might be? Girls!" he said, then he tried to smooch me on the mouth and scuttled off back down the fire-escape, with the cigarette wagging in the corner of his grinning face. I stayed up until sunset.

I was thinking about girls, though. One girl in particular. I'm going to call her Jasmine, partly because that is her actual name, and partly, therefore, to double-bluff you into thinking that if there's one name this girl might have, it certainly isn't Jasmine. Jasmine our secret is safe. I met Jasmine a while back, both of us doing this dumb meet-and-greet job, most of the time all we had to do was sit around in an empty lobby and wait for the shifts of folks to come in or out of a conference room. Very easy. They gave us edgy but serious uniforms—skirt a little on the short side, if you want my opinion—art-business smart you might say, lots of graphite and black. Jasmine was sitting across from me, up on the counter of the bar, and I caught a glimpse of her underwear. Bright red. I'd never thought about desire before. I certainly hadn't thought about Jasmine as the object of my desire, but that one glance at her sitting so demurely did it, I knew I just wanted to lie down and touch the soft velvet of her. Not even sex, really, just to cup around her and smell her hair. Eventually, yes, obviously, sex too, but I was kind of lost in the moment. Call me romantic. At any rate, I stopped talking. Maybe my idiot mouth hung open. I don't know, maybe I was drooling. Jasmine started laughing, and then I started laughing, too. It was only because she started blushing that I knew she knew why I'd stopped talking, but she wasn't mad at me. That's another reason why I loved Jasmine. We didn't have to talk about these things. I thought I was busted, but we still walked back to the subway together, and just before we got there, she took my hand in hers, and we walked along secretly like that; like spies or something. We both went to our separate homes that night, too, but we'd crossed some bridge. Result was, I end up sitting on the rooftop watching the starlings whirl, while my brother laughs at my brainlessness. I was way behind on the respect scales. But I didn't care. There's a lot of other things I could say about Jasmine, or Jasmine and me, but I won't. Not because she's not remarkable and entirely her own person, but because she's herself, and has her own rhythms and tides that I don't control or even want to control. I was aware, though, that all of these suspicious behaviors had crept into me, things that other people didn't do, or didn't automatically do. I can't pin them all on my brother. Maybe we're all just getting more and more suspicious these days. Playing those wonderful games, like I'd get on the train, but wait until the doors began closing; then jump off, but immediately jump back on again, clocking the platform to see if anyone is following or watching. Or take three trains, doubling back twice like that, wouldn't once do? But would once do, really? When I look at it from the here and now, I wonder how I could have lucked out, how I could have accidentally picked up those traits of invisibility. It certainly wasn't anything to do with prudence: I liked the excitement of the dance involved in a phantom chase, and I did it all the time, since I was small; before hi-tech games, before enhanced lenses, before my brother's 'training', and definitely before Kobi. But I never mentioned Kobi to Jasmine, or Jasmine to Kobi. It was clear as Paleolithic water that the two most important people in my life shouldn't know any details about each other. Strawberry propagation. Guerrilla cells. I was only the transmitter of incomplete messages, never really comprehending them myself, giving them out and passing them on before they were needed, or after they were even useful. Maybe, running the wrong ways through time, the right messages, sadly in the incorrect direction. I don't even pretend to know. How do you deal with a person who believes they are living backwards?

I'm sitting with Kobi at the end of a platform, another one, a different one, always a different one. Maybe after long enough, I could work out where the next one would be simply by working out which ones we'd never been to? But there's thousands of platforms, in every direction, and in the end, we met what? only about twenty or thirty times. Yet, here we are, sitting, seated, when a particularly noisy train pulls in. Kobi stops talking, and the train pulls out, with a sound of shearing metal. But Kobi doesn't carry on. Then, a whine in the distance, a clattering, and the express tears in from the other direction, rattling through, red lights fade, and rounding the curve, silence. "That's what I'm talking about. You think you've got it figured, then it just whips through from the other direction and flattens you."

He was squinting at me, holding up his arm to shade his face from the lamps across the tracks, when I noticed his pupils were completely dilated. Almost as though he didn't have any. I'd assumed his eyes were brown, but on closer examination, they didn't seem to have any color at all.

"Are your eyes OK?"

"Yeah, they're fine, they don't work much in the bright."

He made a vague gesture at the ceiling, up there, past there, to where the sun shines.

"Don't close down proper, you know? I'd have to really concentrate."

Then he looked into my eyes, and I swear, I've never seen anyone do this before or since, he made a little pause and his irises started closing of their own accord. They were green. I almost fell off the seat when, abruptly, they sprang back open again—deep, dark pupils, like wells, and he had to go back to the squint.

"You can do that? People can't do that. You can't control it."

"Well, I didn't say I could control it. Takes a lot of out you, you know."

That at least explained why he stayed underground. He'd have no chance up top during the day.

"Has its compensations: I can see pretty well in the dark. If I keep eating my carrots..." and he collapsed into a coughing fit. He might have been laughing.

He was gasping for air now, drawing it in and out like he'd been running up ten flights of stairs. No squash ball, but fist pumping nervously; clutching, squeezing the air. The thought did cross my mind that maybe he was doing all his breathing on manual, as it were. He'd stopped talking and was looking pained, leaning crooked over with his chest on his knees; the closest I got to hear him complain.

"You OK?"

In reply he patted my leg and we sat there until the next train roared in, the next crowds intermingled, and the train roared off again. I looked both ways, I listened both ways, I imagined listening down every tunnel, straining for the quietest sounds, the ones that small animals might notice, or sudden slight shifts of steel might produce. Listened off into the future for the next train, and the next one, or the replay of the train which had last pulled away. The rush of blood through my ears, the beating of my heart, the wheezings of Kobi, simmering down, the metal heel of a shoe clacking on the tiled platform, just one.

The unsilent silence.

"Why were you in hospital?"

"Why? Because I was dead."

Jasmine, on the other hand.... if I could only use one word to describe her, it would be 'alive'. Things moved ahead pretty fast after that. I mean, we had a kiss and everything. And got rid of that gig, well it got rid of us and everybody else, because that was so last week, and this week's crowd were looking for next week's thing, so: go home. But now we needed a place of our own even more, I mean I could hardly take Jasmine home with me, could I? for one thing my brother would probably hit on her, and hanging out in subway tunnels didn't seem particularly 'her'. I wanted a place where we could lie down together out of the cold, and as it turned out, she had one of her own.

I have to back up here a little bit, because I already knew about where a person could go, part-time, cut-price, half asleep and reasonably safe, but the edges shifted constantly, and the difference between tolerated and forbidden wasn't exactly posted on the fence. Over in Gowanus, an entire part of the city had been flattened, waiting for some development or other, but that was when everyone was high on the hog, and in betweentimes, the bottoms had fallen out of all the schemes, and the area was nothing more than a shifting mess of temporary buildings, railroad spurs, off-ramps leading nowhere, or back from nowhere, and mountains and mountains of empty or abandoned shipping containers. From time to time, you'd hear that there was a space available in one sector, or a timeshare in another. And we really are talking containers here, not dwellings in anything like a meaningful sense. Literally a box, or half a box that you could lock up and hide away in; or cut a hole through with an oxy torch and temporarily enter this three-dimensional maze.

There were dangers attached and it was uncomfortable as hell, but a lot of interesting people moved through, too, and absolutely no-one knew who was where, or what they were doing or why. I'd been angling to find something for at least as long as I knew about the place, and now, well, it transpired that Jasmine had a pad there that I was welcome to use. Sometimes. Gowanus is Hell. But yes but, we were the true denizens of this Hell, and we weren't such bad people, mostly. The main complaints, in fact, were sissy complaints, mostly that there was lousy coverage under the flyovers, between the endless angled walls of steel, a badger burrow megalopolis of Faraday cages. Which meant almost nothing electronic worked properly down there, almost no reception at all, almost all of the time. Which, paradoxically, also meant no, or almost no transmission, ever, perhaps interference? And that, my friends, is what must have accidentally saved me. That and the joy I felt at the myriad ways of getting in and out of the place. Someone had an algorithm for it, but the best and most accurate description I ever heard was that there might be many ways into Gowanus, but how many ways are there out of it? The answer is: more than you think.

Right now, I have to pause, to take a breath from telling you this story, because I am beginning to feel overwhelmed. I look at my life, my actual life, and it seems to be composed of tatters, ragged flags and strips of material flapping in a wind from all directions. Not that any of the scraps in and of themselves are particularly disturbing, or that I don't have a great affection for some of the threads, but they are not tied together, not sewn, and never have been. I am tempted to say that they never will be, either, and I am O.K. with that, we can't always expect that our lives will add up to anything more than those few parts of a few brief tatters, anyway. But there's an unease I sense now, that some of these fragments don't even belong to the story of my life, I'm skating across a cold patch in someone else's life and mistaking my time with them for their (brief) time with me, which is not at all the same thing, and this unease, Kobi would say, is because I feel the pressure wave of a future, of futures, which aren't mine, coming down the tunnels at me, backing up the air and making me worry 'What's wrong now?'; nothing's wrong now, it's 'What's not wrong yet'... and it may be in my life, it may be in a part of my life, or it may be in the next tunnel, in someone else's life, and all I am doing is feeling the cold wind of their catastrophe brush over the skin of my arm, and then I'll be fine, the cold spell will pass, but they'll be gone, with the red tail-lights. Such now.

Jasmine was keen for me to get the lenses out. Games weren't her thing anyway, not that kind. If anything, she was addicted to the physical world. Her parents had been Jaïns, and some of that had rubbed off on her in a rebellious way, she was so gentle. We'd agreed to meet at her hideaway, and to show willing, and that I wasn't a complete imbecile, I brought some eggs, a bottle of borax eyewash, some cotton pads, and those cleansing tips you are not supposed to stick in your ears. The idea was to soak my eyes in the wash, gently and painlessly peel the coverings away, and then leave the eyes fallow for a few days. Truth be told, I was starting to have the heebie-jeebies about worms. I grabbed a gallon jar of distilled rainwater from the convenience automat and climbed through the chain link into north Gowanus.

Jasmine's sleeping cube was about a mile from the edge, dead center, as the crow flies—though I'm not a crow—and about twice as far as the rat runs, so I started the long climb, aiming for the central pillar of the I-278 flyover above the canal. The containers on the north and east sides had been deposited in a more or less orderly fashion, and thus abandoned in a more or less orderly way. There were holes punched out where some assiduous owner had insisted their orphan container be removed, and these holes had been shored up with woodblocks and pilings, sometimes with steel supports and girders, but always overhung by the next layer up, or makeshift ladders. The liveries of the various companies were randomly piled one on the next, with some interesting cluster effects—here a rash of pinks and salmons; there turquoises and lilacs, going up ten to fifteen layers, and then over the top stretching off westward for another two miles to the bay, way beyond Gowanus proper, out almost to the hospital. Out there, the entire edifice had teetered over, and containers were always tumbling into the bay, open to the elements, scuttled with rodents, and home to the most unsavory characters. Jasmine had the use of half a container, on the edge of what I'd call the civilized part, with the entrance via a hand-cut, lockable hatch on the top. Inside, there was a sidewall cut into the adjacent container, invisible from the outside, which a bunch of people used communally, then other shafts would take you into the depths, though some of the lower bins had rusted out and were waterlogged, so weren't used even by runaways. Needless to say, the whole Republic was a no-go area, and needless to say, no-one would look out for you if you couldn't look out for yourself. Honor among thieves? give me a break. But there were rules, complicated 'secret' handshakes, or gestures, clans in territories as small as three containers, or as big as a quarter mile cube, where someone had Authority, and you'd better know Who or you'd be in trouble, and as anyone with half a brain would tell you, it's not who you know, it's who knows you, so gently, gently, catch a mousey, this is where I was going to carefully convalesce, or have to be quickly dragged blind to the eye hospital if something went wrong. I wasn't in the best of moods when I dropped into the hatch and found Jasmine waiting, fixing up her xmas tree lights lights with a bunch of empty springwater bottles, throwing that blue over everything, as though I was simply coming over for tea and scones. I'm no Luddite, or even fancy about things, but I never liked those little l.e.d. lights, they're so cold and unwavering. Give me an incandescent every time, even a dim one. But guess what? Jasmine had taken care of that, too. She'd found one of those filament bulbs, only about twenty watts, dim and glorious. There was the mattress roll, bedding, neatly bundled, a couple of crates, her metal chest, and a pile of clothes in the corner, all folded on a tatami. All very oriental. And the hatch locked from the inside, in our own little submarine. Jasmine took a look at my medical provisions and threw a fit. Did I tell you she was a witch? Well, how was I to know? She ripped into the items I'd bought and pulled out her own remedies that she had ready and waiting. Just to prove I'm not making it all up, I'm going to include the recipe here, let me tell you, that fifth ingredient surprised me, but when you put your life and health and safety in the hands of a nineteen-year-old *bruja*, you have to be prepared for a little shock, awe and pain. She knew what she was doing though. Or, thank the stars, the *abuelita* she had been sneakily watching all her life knew what she was doing.

Jasmine's Abuela's eyewash recipe from India

Eyebright—*Euphrasia officinalis*—1 part / ¼ cup
Bayberry Root bark—*Myrica pensylvanica*—1 part / ¼ cup
Red Raspberry leaf—*Rubus idaeus*—1 part / ¼ cup
Goldenseal—*Hydratis canadensis*—1 part / ¼ cup
Cayenne pepper—*Capsicum annuum*—1/10th part / 1 tsp.

Infuse I tsp. mixture in 12 fl.oz. boiling water
ALLOW TO COOL BEFORE APPLYING.
Infusion may also be drunk, hot or iced.

First, Jasmine looked at the state of play of my eyes. I admit I had been rubbing and grubbing at them unnecessarily since I'd decided to take the plunge, so they were a nice map of reds and inflammation. The general idea was to keep flooding the eye with fluid, and slowly tease up the edges of the lens, preferably without detaching any of the cornea, it isn't something you can do by yourself. Accordingly, I lay my head back and let her get on with it. That retro bulb helped, everything faded into a liquid brown blur, and the borax didn't sting too much. But that turned out to be simply because Jasmine hadn't begun the jimmying yet. Even when she did, it didn't start off too bad, I think the darkness helped, and her humming, and the fact that I really wanted to be brave or at least not appear a whiny brat because I got my privileged toys stuck in my eyes. And then suddenly it was over, lifted off with barely a twinge, and she popped the first contact into a jar, flushed away, and went straight over to eye two. Same story here, but with more teasing and tweaking. I was getting to enjoy the feel of Jasmine's body leaning over me. She was so determined and absorbed, and she kept asking if I was O.K., if she was hurting me, and saying sorry if she nicked me as she carefully worked the lenses loose. The warmth of her leaning on my chest was the best anaesthetic you could have. Then, the second one came out. I couldn't believe it. I could still see, and apart from a slight tingle, there seemed to be no harm done.

"O.K." she said, "now this might sting a little." You remember that fifth ingredient I talked about up there? Well, whoever had the idea of putting cayenne pepper into raw eyes is either a sadist, or knows something about eye tissue that I don't. Because it stung like bejaysus, like being sprayed by the cops or one of those stevia vigilantes who think you're going to eat their tiny mental-support-dog if you look at them sideways. But in it went. She'd made them into teabags. One onto each eye, steeped in hot water. How can you put hot water into someone's eye? That part I mentioned about not wanting to seem like a wuss. I'm not sure if the things I said to her were going to endear her to me. Then again, as ever, they were in my own private language, so what you don't understand you don't really hear, right?

I spent the rest of the night and the whole next day whimpering on her bed, sometimes she leant against the wall looking at me, sometimes she lay down and spooned me. I wasn't thinking erotic thoughts at all. My eyes got worse and worse, as though the entire front had been ripped off. They hadn't, but that's what it felt like. And do you know the only thing that worked to soothe them? Egg whites. Then back on the teabags. Like a Proper English Breakfast, all it needed was the baked beans, and my eyes could open a Proper English café.

When we went out the next evening, to catch the last of the daylight, I couldn't bear to even glance at the sky. Jasmine made me, though, and held up a mirror so I could examine the scarring across the whites of my eyes, like the craters on the moon. She had put the contacts into her grandmother's magic tea potion. I left them floating, in her box, and sulked in the corner feeling sorry for myself. Never again. Until the next time. The politics of neediness.

Then there were a few Golden Days.

My eyes were recovering slowly, looking less like an archipelago, and more like I'd been drinking too much. Jasmine bought me some golden sunglasses, even the wraparound was golden, like a spaceboy's faceplate, and made everything bend itself reflect off our heads like a giant world shaped smile. We sat on the precarious stacks and looked out over the Bay, the Navy Yards, over there, the Narrows Bridge on the horizon, Manhattan rising out of the sea. Perfect days. Perfect nights, leaving the hatch open, baking, while I stretched out behind Jasmine, and curled over her body, limbs entangled, her ass filling the curve of my hips, my hands reaching over to her shoulders, pulling her to me, her back pressing against my chest, I could stroke her breasts and pretend they were my own, bury my nose into her hair and breathe her in, and she could do the same to me.

I didn't go home, why would I go home when we were the Royal Couple of Gowanus. Monarch butterflies, readying for the migration, led by the breeze off the sea, out to Far Rockaway, Gee's Bend, and on beyond Yucatan.

The astronaut glasses were for Kobi. It was topping one hundred degrees unless you could find shade and a breeze, and the tunnels were hotter than that, burnt and airless. He was reluctant. But I could see it was something he was itching to do. The glasses were the clincher in trade for coming outdoors. He looked like some proto-funk star. But the thing is, they actually did what it said on the tin, and blocked out ninety-five percent of sunlight. He could stand it. We sat up in the foliage on the High Line and looked out to Jersey.

The other thing is, Kobi's completely nuts. He's in his own element down by the tracks, but up top, he's completely lost, he comes over all giddy, like he needs a seeing eye dog even if he's the opposite of blind, in fact he gets overwhelmed by movement and light. He keeps dodging things which aren't even there, or they are there, in his field of vision, but three streets away. Helicopters darting overhead would make him duck. I had to get him to sit still, and we had a time tracing the movement of gulls, trying to work out their schedules. I told him gulls didn't have schedules, but he insisted they did, well, not schedules as such, but he would observe them for a while, then start to work out their flightpaths, almost as if he were conducting them, and sure enough, he could predict when one would glide down and land, when another would take off, and when others would hover and glide, or bank off to the river. It seemed to calm him and made him laugh.

"So fast! The birds...!" Laughing at the seagulls, or the clusters of sparrows. I wished I'd brought some breadcrumbs.

Kobi surprised me that day, firstly because he's utterly familiar with the city. I'd thought he spent all his time huddled up underground, but that's only in the winter, apparently. The rest of the year he wanders around on foot, and knows all the short-cuts, all the alleyways, and seems completely up-to-date on road-works and new developments. He kept pointing out bland buildings or street-corners and saying things like "That used to be a watering hole for big cats," or "The first canal across town goes right under that bank." That's how I worked out that he never sleeps. I thought he must have a bunk or a niche in some side tunnel of the subway system. But he wanders around like a manta ray and keeps in motion. Gotta keep the blood circulating. Anyway, secondly, what he told me as we dragged around midtown was that he's not actually a human being, but some strain of Artificial Intelligence. I can be sensitive to that, and from what he knows and the way he behaves I might be inclined to believe him; but then again, if someone looks like a human being and presents as a human being, I am willing to give them the benefit of the doubt that way, too. But he says he's not. It is probably some deliberately vague Grand Metaphor on the condition of sentient beings. He claims to come from "up there". As he spoke those words we were climbing, haltingly, the broad staircase near Chelsea Market, and pausing while he recaught his breath. "Up there," and a wave of the hand around the pencil-thin skyscrapers that were fashionable at that time.

I thought his gesture hinted he was a space-alien, but no, it meant the strings and wires, power lines and rails, machines, soul-of-the-city that runs through every structure, circuit, water and gas main, every street and sewer. It did occur to me that he was speaking quite literally, and that he considered all of us nothing more than information sway, but that's not correct, either; that he was a leftover fragment of the artificial intelligence system that is the city, so he knew what he was talking about, right?

When he burst into this world, one chilly day in a hospital intensive care unit, connected to all manner of devices, he had to work out how to operate his body before the doctors turned the life-support machines off. His machines now. Well, that's his mythology. I couldn't think of anything intelligent to say, being still unsure if he wasn't the latter-day equivalent of those guys in the looney bins who professed lineage to Napoleon, or John the Baptist; or women claiming to be Joan of Arc, or Lilith; and who would argue till the cows came home about the weird *you-wouldn't-believe-me-if-I-told-you-but-I'm-going-to-tell-you-anyway* list of reasons how they simply and surely knew they were the reincarnation of some Emperor, Prince, or Great Warrior, and never, but never, a serf or a slave, or a tubercular peasant from the Middle Ages. I had zero idea where Kobi got his information from, but I didn't want to look like I was trashing his story either, or undermining him in the slightest way—because everybody needs a story—and because he knew so much stuff, most of which turned out to be true, in the end.

He liked the sunglasses, anyway, so I let him keep them. And left him up there, a dot of negative space in a stream of people, leaning back in golden rays and soaking up the last Indian Summer sun, while I rushed home to my belovèd, crushed together in a steel can under a highway bridge in the ancient borough of Kings.

Something has happened. I don't know even if I can tell you about it. Like all violence, it comes out of nowhere, I mean, never out of nowhere, but you don't know it's coming, so it seems out of nowhere, and it arrives fast, it leaves fast, and it's entirely random. Like some raven that lights on your shoulder to peck your eyes out, like in the proverb; or maybe it doesn't peck your eyes out this time, and you wonder why not? then it flies off again. Because it wasn't your turn today, maybe next time? You're standing there in shock, it's already quiet again, but something's changed, something's missing, something's gone. And sometimes you can glue the pieces together, and sometimes you can't, it doesn't really matter in the scheme of things, and I don't even know if it helps, it's just an intuition we cling to, so we don't believe it will happen to us, but the truth is, we missed it last time, we missed it this time, so we'll miss it next time, too.

I only know these things because they happened to me.

I'd been spending more and more time with Jasmine, or poking around the container park, and less and less time at home, and that maybe freed them up a little too, because when I did go back, life seemed a little more serene, mine and theirs. That's the problem with time, it flows to its own design, and we bob along like corks, never suspecting there's a whirlpool around the next leisurely meander. Or maybe you do feel the undertow, without knowing exactly why you feel uneasy or breathless, and afterwards call it instinct or premonition. I didn't have a premonition, though. I was relaxing, I'd let myself go on a sunny afternoon, strolled across the city to my mother's place, and left Jasmine to get on with her understated polyamory. I didn't have any problems with her seeing other people, but it was a closet of a room, and I think I was too in love with the inconsequentiality of just being with her, without having to do anything. I wasn't keen on some random guy sharing our bed. I admit a third person makes me uncomfortable, almost a question of cleanliness, like three people sharing one toothbrush. And the gentle stuff, things like long silences, always disappears when there is another body around. So, I went back home to Mom, lived and learned, no big deal.

My brother could tell straight away that I'd been having some issues with my eyes, but he disguised it from our mother by affecting to praise my sunglasses, turning them over in his hands approvingly while he was really examining my eyes. I blinked and let him look, then he handed the glasses back. I'd left his precious hi-end contacts in Jasmine's fridge, in her Mason jar, no way was I walking around the city with that kind of hardware jangling loose in my backpack. Then it was like a sampling of an idyllic afternoon, but somehow all slotted together from stock footage. The smell of the coffee, a shaft of sunlight, some birds flying over, a siren, a sigh from my mother, my brother curling out a smoke ring, which hung in the atmosphere, or did it? I've forgotten the beauty, because I've replayed the entire film in my head too many times now.

The front door resonated with an almighty thud, and we all, in slow motion, looked over. It wasn't a knock, more like a truck had crashed into the corridor wall, twelve flights up. My brother had reinforced that door—they were called 'bailiff proof'; a special lock, iron bars sliding up and sideways into a steel frame. But as we watched, to another thud we felt in our bellies, there was a ratcheting sound, and the entire door peeled back off its hinges like a sardine can opened with a key. The hinges popped out and the door folded back on itself at a right angle. And in they came. Not police, not army, but not *not* the police and not *not* the army, neither. I don't know how many square guys in black suits and helmets, five? six? more outside. They jogged straight in, not in too much of a hurry, and grabbed the three of us. First, they got to my mother, twisted her head around, and leant over her face; then I got grabbed, a gloved hand damned near crushed my jaw, and the goon shone this really bright flashlight thing into my eyes, took a good look at what he saw, then threw me to the floor like I was a pet toy. Then they yanked the door of the fridge open, and rifled the contents, smashing everything on the floor, all the jars of *frito* my mother had made, the sad half cartons of juice no-one had thrown out, eggs, it looked like everything fragile in our lives was in that fridge, maybe we should have all crawled in earlier, much earlier, and pulled the door shut behind us.

I could hear my brother yelling, he'd put up half a second's extra struggle, or maybe he was just furthest from the door, anyway, he didn't make the window or the fire escape, and I heard him say an obscenity, which even under the shock made me laugh, proud, that he could use the proper verb form (which wasn't always the case) even in such tense circumstances. Then the cube-shaped guys hit him a few times and pinned him down and gave him the same scan they'd given the rest of the family, only this time, in his case, they didn't throw him down like a ragdoll. They kind of gave each other some coded signal, photo-flashed the scanner in his eyes, then it looked like they stabbed him with the end of it. My brother screamed, and I had this sudden image—one I never even half-remembered until then—of my brother's father, a greasy slob as far as I knew, that was the guy, sitting in a park and sharing a cigar with my brother. His first cigar. He must have been nine or ten, which makes me about four. No cigar for me. I wasn't *his* kid, too young, and well, not anything to do with manly things like bonding with your macho son and smoking cigars. My mother was behaving like a simpering idiot, too, bringing drinks and snacks and stuff for the guy. The thing he used, though, his weird little fetish tool, swift and decisive, to cut the end off the cigar, more or less, is what these fuckers used to clip my brother's optics out. They happened to clip the front of his eyes, too.

One. Two. Punched him professionally once more in the face for good measure, dropped the retrieved lenses in a tube, put the tube in a bag, sealed it, looked around at their little visit's chaos, and left. Backed out and vanished.

I was having trouble with sound. It had gone, it was all moving outside of my senses, my ears and my eyes certainly did not want to register what had just gone down. But I knew my brother had not stopped screaming, in many ways he hadn't even started. The whole episode took maybe half a minute. And we were done, even if we were all still alive. It was only money. No crime, no justice, no retribution, no revenge; nothing more than a dull retrieval of property. And now we could all go back to enjoying our pleasant afternoon.

My brother was thrashing around on the floor, knocking everything over. The neighbors popped their heads round the door, not to help, you understand, but to slink off once they'd made sure they themselves were OK. My brother was trying to find his telephone, which I shoved into his hands, but he couldn't dial, so slippery with his blood, and his jerky movements, so I dialed for him. No medics (how could we even imagine affording medics?!) Find some way to get him out of there to his famous so-called 'friends & comrades.' 'His comrades'? No way they were going to come near him after this, but maybe we could get to his friends.

Thus began my second life as my brother's keeper.

Getting him down the emergency stairs, his face covered in a scarf, without anyone seeing him, and he, obviously, seeing nothing at all, was done in the same daze. No time passed, we were already out in the haze, ordinary people walking by in their ordinary lives. A taxi suddenly pulled over, and many panicked hands dragged my brother inside. Reality proceeding via cuts. Splices.

I was left on the streetcorner, on my own. The noises of the city came back, slowly, the air was cool, a slight breeze, I couldn't go home, I didn't know where my brother was, or what state he was in except he was still alive, and that there was no rowing back from the fact that he was now sightless and would forever remain that way. Also, that we, as a family or individuals could in no way remain in that apartment, and that soon enough, other people, maybe less aggressively, maybe not, would be coming to collect on the debt. The landlords would have some other suckers in by the weekend, and bill us for the twisted door, too: bye-bye the six months deposit.

Talk about premonitions, though, as I stood there, I realized that the violence had gone. It simply wasn't there anymore. It was a beautiful day, and everyone was still alive. Even the guys who'd committed the violence probably weren't being violent right at that moment, they were probably in the back of their van eating snacks; or maybe gearing up to make another raid, then home to the kids for a shower and a bonus. Where had all that dark energy gone back to? I had absolutely no idea what to do at all. So, I sat back against the railings of a children's park until I was capable of standing up without falling over, staring at my feet. Everyone left me alone, of course they did.

When it was dark, I ran straight to find Kobi, and it was as though he had my number, because this time, there he was, sitting, staring at me the moment I entered his platform. He stood up and motioned me to follow him, while I had no chance to get a single word out of the script I'd been running all the way in my head, what I was going to tell him, what I was going to ask, what I was supposed to do, Kobi stepped off the platform, down the few steps, and shuffled off into the tunnel hugging close to the wall, as though he already knew, which, in fact, he did. I followed him down into the labyrinth like it was the most natural thing in the world. Here I am, half a mile beneath New York City, with a crazy old black man who can hardly walk and seems to think he's dead, anyway. He's not dead, he's walking. And I'm in a daze, stumping along behind him, wondering how I can't keep up, and what I can do about this awful hole that's been punched in my life.

I could see Kobi was in his element here, he knew how to dance over the sleepers, and obviously how to dodge the trains, duck down side-culverts and up little half-ladders, until we got to a niche, maybe something once used to stack boxes or coils of cable, but now empty. Some sheets of folded carboard to ease the harshness of the lumpy floor, and cover the puddles we squatted in. If my life were a film, this part would have no soundtrack, and you'd have to learn to lip read to find out what we talked about, but you can guess what we were talking about, I wanted to know what I could possibly ever do about my brother, and whether it was ever going to be safe to go home, or how I could get back to Jasmine's, assuming she'd done with her sex exercises for the day.

But Kobi wasn't interested in talking or putting up with my blather. He just covered me with his filthy blankets, rolled up something soft under my head, and sat guard while the trains screeched past; the rainwater, or river sludge infiltrated drip by drip; and the scuttling noises and eyes in the corners revealed themselves not as predators, but as kindred spirits, warm, warm in their animal wellbeing.

I have no idea how long I slept, but when I awoke, Kobi had gone. Remarkably, I found I could steer my way by the subterranean starlight—reflections, signals, dim bulbs spliced irregularly into frayed wiring. Once outside, seamlessly carried into the flow of the crowds, origins lost, up the staircases and into the air. Daylight. Now what?

No follow-up on the raid ever materialized, like a summer thunderstorm that never breaks. My brother did not get an infection, instead, he became alarmingly calm, I'd thought he would be raging and bitter, but no, he sat around, head tilted to one side, listening for liminal sounds I couldn't hear, or leant out of the window to breathe in the airs and endless wash of noise. The other thing was we both moved out to under the thruway, more or less nomadic, never staying anywhere more than a few nights. I was looking after him full time now. And that's how I got his old job in the Xartel, running merchandise and messages (and sometimes waters) from here to there and back again. It brought in money, and no-one could touch me for speed and discretion. I think it gave the guys a blast to have somehow managed to keep it in the family, me being the pipsqueak, and all. Jasmine and I were ancient history by now, though we'd bump into each other from time to time, sometimes quite literally rushing round a corner between shipping containers, or going up the down ladders, and we were still nice to each other, saying hello. Once we'd even managed to bring each other off, squeezed into an alcove with our hands in each other's pants, while people walked right by a few feet away, leaning into each other and breathing each other's breath, murmuring in each other's ears, for old times' sake, and it was nice to hold each other there, for one calm moment, though we both knew those times had long long gone, but mainly because Jasmine's a sunny girl and she naturally veers away from any darkness—I hear she finally cracked and works as a virtual tour guide these days—while I move in a pretty dark world even if, to my own surprise, I don't feel particularly dark. Probably smoking too much mica.

I hadn't seen or sought out Kobi for nearly three months when it finally occurred to me.

I went back to the high-line, end of November, but bright, bright sun. And there he was, sitting in the exact same spot I'd left him those months before, with his astro-glasses on.

"Do I know you?" is what he barked at me, curling a pointed finger.

I nodded, decisively, I hope.

"What's my name?"

"I don't know. I always called you Kobi."

While he mulled this over, he was gazing off at a building sized poster for the Port Authority.

YOU CAN GET ANYWHERE FROM THE PORT AUTHORITY

It said that on the poster, in letters twenty feet high, right behind him.

MORE THAN TWO MILLION JOURNEYS A YEAR START HERE

Now, everyone has a narrative, and I usually let them get on with it. What happens if you call them out is awkward and strange to behold, they'll only dig deeper into their Big Lie, it's not possible they'll ever just say, OK, you're right, it's all nonsense. And I was not, emphatically not, going to do that to Kobi, but, for my own weak reasons, I wanted to know, if his tall stories really were true, or could be admitted true in some way, to humor him, as it were, if he wasn't scared at the next step? or sad to be leaving someone, something, *anything* behind.

Kobi put the tips of his fingers together and thought about that for some time.

All he said was, "Blue." By which I think he meant not simply the intellectual concept of blueness, but every one of the tints and shades and hues that might variously be subsumed under the single word 'Blue'. One among the million millions that had no reason to be, and were thus unimaginable until you did experience them, then, undeniably.

At least, that's what I think he meant. He could just have meant it made him feel sad.

Then he straightened his back, rummaged in his coat pocket, and pulled out what was left of his busted squash ball.

"You never did tell me your name."

This is where they'll get you, every time. Names.

"Miranda. My name is Miranda."

"Pleased to meet you, Miranda.

With which, he placed the ball in the palm of my hand, lay back flat on the bench, crossed his arms on his chest like a pharaoh, and gave up his struggle with breathing.

This is the idea I'd been nurturing for Kobi.

First, I'd call the medics. Then I'd lean over Kobi, and take Jasmine's jar out of my Faraday cage backpack. Then I'd carefully place those forbidden tech lenses into Kobi's eyes. They'd be fully charged, and about as well-connected as it's possible to be on this planet.

Then, when I heard the medics arriving with their charge cart and cables and tubes, I'd put my lips close to Kobi's ear and quietly say:

"You are fully online now, Mister Kobi. Good luck."

Then I'd walk right out of there.

I always love monsoon season. If you can manage to stay warm and dry. Nobody goes out, and even those who do look straight ahead and get on with their business. I've found a few vantage points overlooking the bay, all the pastel shades of the containers washed in that textured pulse of rain on steel. I can sit up here, huddled against a pillar of the overhead thruway, and let the sound and the fierceness of the rain lash all around me, smoke a mica cigarette, and let go of the burden for a moment.

I like to imagine that Kobi made it back into his mythical world of grids and lines, or that one old guy finally found some peace. The genuine Napoleon safely back on his island.

Even I can find peace, up here, in the driving rain, looking across the blurred waters, with a couple of smokes.

While a few storeys below me, overhanging the water, my idiot-savant brother dances out over the void, a barefoot trapeze artiste on barefoot girders, navigating his new way around the universe with his hearing and his balance and the soles of his feet. Some kind of Saint.

It's so beautiful, in spite of everything.

Almost as if it were all real.

the one about the jigsaws

THE RAILROAD TRACKS pass right by the south side of the building. Old building. New roof. New elevators, new composite floors. *Terrazzo*. Or Marmoreal. I'm not sure. I got the ground floor. Street level. Even then, there's a disabled persons' access ramp outside the front door, taking you down to the sidewalk. Also *terrazzo*. Which is very calming for everyone, except those who have orange/green Daltonism. For whom it's a soft terror. You shouldn't always be staring at the floor anyway is what I say. Especially if you have orange/green Daltonism. You know, the traffic lights are arranged vertically for exactly that reason. Up means Stop. Down means Go. It was a newly opened refurbished post-industrial space for *artistes* and freelancers. Also Section Eight people with non-violent case histories. As far as anyone could know until the full Police State sets itself up.

Pliss state yr bizniss. Until then: gossip, rumor, and innuendo. Looking askance and throwing the stink-eye. On neighbors. Absent partners, with their violet stories. Recently refurbished but still I'd managed not to be the first tenant. She'd been let go. Probably not a suicide, the official language would have been other. And the *terrazzo* might have needed a re-buffing. Still, I ran my fingernails along the brass tile separators, just to check.

CSI trick. I'm not a forensic scientist, I just watch a lot of macabre and badly plotted shows. I suspect the writers of the shows aren't forensic scientists either, to judge by their grasp of any other scientific principles such as air-drag, gravity or basic thermodynamics. Genetics. But I digress. My own grasp of such things is so out of date now, when every girl and her dog can quote the laws and quirks of quantum mechanics as they blow bubbles softly into their *maté* glasses.

I had managed to move into the complex during its first ninety days. The mailbox in the ¿witty? atrium designed to look like, or scavenged from, some nineteen-twenties Post Office. The little decorative mailbox key a nice touch, too, for those of us sensitive to design detail. The mailbox, then, always stuffed with anonymous or misdirected mail. Sometimes *currentresident* but more and more *fionawakefield,* general offers of credit cards, once-in-a-lifetime opportunities, but also more and more shrill unpaid bills, official *forwardingservicerequested* windowed envelopes, and tapering according to the usual Gaussian bellcurve, past the outliers and then nothing for the past three weeks. Until this morning.

Hand-written address *fionawakefield* and tiny, tiny return address P.O.Box label in the upper left. Yellow. Manila. Padded. I doubt very much that bananas are still used in their manufacture. Pictorial current issue postage stamp. A nice touch. Jimi Hendrix's face. Or hemp. No-one had ever met *fionawakefield* or would admit to having met her. I only bring it up because I had the devil's own time to get the utilities connected because the company insisted I must know *fionawakefield* because she'd only recently moved in. I didn't. The company didn't understand that people can have also only recently moved out. Or been moved out, if

I may stoop to use another passive construction. The housing association wouldn't give me any information at all and why should they, as I wasn't—by my own admission—a relative. I took the mail to their offices for the first few weeks, then gave up and just threw it away. After all, I was now *currentresident*. And though the post office wasn't far away, it was still far enough to require that I put on clothes of some kind, some outdoors kind, and boots, and generally spruce myself up, also take a coffee, and untousle my hair, maybe have a shave. It gets complicated being a good neighbor. But this looked like an interesting package. Small, lightweight, but somehow lumpy. Like one of those cheap old sandwiches you could find on Wonderbread, cut in triangles, curling up, or wrapped in waxed paper. All the cheese and butter huddled in the middle of the slice like clergymen in a church with a leaking roof.

Not that I am averse to letting myself go like that, unshaven, unkempt, and out into the bracing world. I could muster a tartan dressing gown if needed. No-one paid much attention anyway, and you can always mutter. The problem with the sidewalks being the proliferation of grasses and weeds bursting hideously through the fissures and gaps. Still today, my version of ballet, to keep the arches dropping down on the cracks between flagstones, the feet turned in, or turned out, parallel or perpendicular to, all the while keeping up a pleasant rhythm, a stride, a walking, nonchalant and driven by the nerve ganglia in the hips, like a little dinosaur, a little like a dinosaur. All to return the mail, unforwardable, of an unknown and possibly apocryphal previous co-tenant. My Ur-tenant, who tainted me from day one with suspicion. Had I known her? Why had I not known her? I must be a friend of hers. Surely? And sub-letting is illegal. I had been on the waiting list for seven years. Perhaps I'd bumped her off. Perhaps she got pregnant. No children allowed in the building. As so often, none of the above, but the questions had already been asked, suspicions aroused. The weight is in the words. The form demands: Detail the drugs you use, medically or for recreational purposes. It's there in black and white. I say, None. The woman from the housing agency writes down, I can see it, read it upside down, even though I am no forensic handwriting expert. Or maybe I am, in the nicest sense of the word amateur. I make no money off it. The lady from the agency writes down: Denies drug use. That's me all over. And now I am also hoarding the mail of others; a federal offense. Even knowing that fact makes me just a bit forensic, doesn't it? But I was settling in, and people were beginning to pleasantly ignore me as my bodyshape and facial contours became familiar to them. Muttering muttering. No harm in that. Get used to the muttering, then at night the murmurings, the voices and sighs through the walls. The ceilings and floors. Their ceilings, my floor; their floors, my ceiling. Unless I got on my cold hands and bony knees in the summer or winter, but right now in the late winter early spring in the interests of factual honesty and precision, pressed my ear to the floor, or wall,. I never worked out how to safely eavesdrop through the ceiling, off some rickety stepladder, presumably, to listen to the animal music, more often than not also to the white noise building static, a radio off-station, of the pipes, the ducts, the network of tubes, the interlinking, in these old, old structures from the eighteen hundreds, girder and brick, glass brick window-walls, new rubberized roof coverings that drove the landlords mad, all that cost, the mold just sealed under, black mold breaking out in great soggy, oozing udders hanging from the underprotected eaves. Economies. As I say, I was just settling in myself.

If it rains, I can go out, manage to cover fifty feet of pavement, count the paces between the telegraph poles, the steps, left-right. Singing a little song in my head. People on the street, sure, I see them, and they see me, but we are on our own tracks, like the blood in a frog's heart, three-chambered, the claret and the indigo do not mix, because of small spiral reticulations of the ventricle. Just so, we walk the same streets, you bear right, I bear left, we lose sight of each other, latch onto some other other, as do they unto us, monkeys swinging from branch to branch, never letting go of the one until the other is at hand. Though eventually we must, to swing is to fly, after all. But, the point I am making is: we are not keeping each other under surveillance, or only for the briefest of moments, the slightest parallelism, then off onto another track, another other, and the illusions of free will and invisibility. Especially in the rain, when those deemed smarter than you or I stay head down under the blankets indoors. Summers, it's more painful and we must look up, needs must, to the clouds the skies. And trip on the irregular unmaintained municipal walkways. Risk that. Back home, to home! Or lurk under bridges, underpasses. People would assume you were there with some purpose, no? When the purpose is to simply stand and listen to the weather. Beating on something. A half-roof. A corrugated shelter. One's own umbrella. Who carries an umbrella?! You find them often, ripped inside out on the carefully gathered mounds of recycled trash like cairns along the roadsides, waiting for the trucks twice a week. And coming back with those steady staples: milk, cheese, bad bread, bad coffee, some edible oil or grease. Bad breath, bad veins, bad teeth, bad heart, bad thoughts.

The envelope sits on the table in front of me, virginally *intacta*. It's a delicious color, that manila. You have a desire to consume it. In the old days, in old-time offices, you could actually indulge such desires, or nurture them, even. The glue has an indefinable taste, also the drag on your lips as you lick across, sharp and sexual, gums and resins, paper-cutting the tongue. A friend, a painter in oils. She shows me Cadmium Yellow, squeezes a little out of the tube onto her fingers, rubs it around, erased beneath essence of Yellow. Yellow. A small gentle snort to herself, for why? Affectionate? Caring? Resigned? Lifts up her sweater, exposes her breast, works the pigment into the flesh, drags her fingers down in a yellow V. Now what? Pull the sweater back down, or pull it over her head? My move. Wool sweater. Pullover. Pull it over, pull you over me. Dizzy. So: manila envelopes, then.

The coffee table is a joke I tell myself, a conceptual and ironic art installation, too low to write on, too cluttered to use for coffee, or food, too hazardous, an ongoing pre-archeological experiment, and a cityscape in miniature, no space to move, the ignored and the forgotten. It's not that big really. Objects promiscuous, innocent of vectors or bounds. So I opened the package to *fionawakefield* and out fell a palm-sized, plastic Ziploc bag. And in the bag, a folded square of paper with a geometric design on it. Circular. Something out of Bosch. Or Breughel; and the pieces of a small jigsaw puzzle. On the exterior of the bag, a graphically mutated letter J and the number one hundred and three, which I noted set off alarm bells in the upper left part of my empty head, it, the number, being a prime. I have something of an allergy or hypersensitivity to primes. Not the low ones, obviously, you won't get very far in this world if you are allergic to two or three or five or seven, for example (although, seven, in fact, is quite the trigger), but the higher ones? Certainly. And one-oh-three is one of them. Outside, the rain still audible, the wired glass blurring the grey skies, dusk falling. The ceiling above as the floor below, guts and innards, the steam pipes susurrate, the walls suppurate. The *terrazzo* tessellates. A pick-up drives by, tires through the water film. A moment's pause, then the train shakes past. A hundred and fifty various wagons and container flatbeds. A mile and a half long, thirty feet away from my bed. Its horn sounds. Two long one short one long. A major second and a perfect fourth. And Katang-katan. Katang-katan. The forks and spoons in the jars on my window ledge rattle in sympathy, dusk is falling, and all is in the well of the world.

Katang-katan. Kanang-danang.

I cleared the coffee table. Wiped it, dried it and spread out the pieces, there must have been about two hundred. First surprise: there were no straight edge pieces. All the few smooth edges were curves. Ergo, the design was circular, perhaps with a thin black border. Second surprise: a slightly spindled stub of paper which read: Be a friend, do not bend. Or rather: BE A FRIEND DO NOT BEND. The pieces were not out-of-the-box new, though in a decent condition. Times like this I wished I smoked but I don't smoke, never have. A few old friends smoked. Used to. A couple of old girlfriends. I always rather liked watching people smoke. Irresponsible of me. A café in Kraków where you couldn't see across the cellar room catapulted me back to the seventies, when every public function would be billowed in cigarette smoke, cigars at Christmas. Even the cinema. Taxis. Upstairs on the bus. Airplanes. Watching a film whose images hung over the audience in sheets, some mediaeval monastery courtyard in Georgia or Azerbaijan, only the last, faintest veil making it onto the whitewashed wall serving as a screen. You'd have to look at everyone's feet to see which way they were facing, or peer back to the projectionist's cabin to find the exit doors. And no-one any the wiser. Sometimes I think people are just monkeys with credit cards. No more basic sense than a sea cucumber, never mind a horse. They have taught monkeys to smoke, too. And they're way overdue on that Shakespeare deal.

The room is never wholly dark at night. It's the one drawback they don't mention in the prospectus. Most people wouldn't mind, anyway. Ordinarily, I would, but I've become used to the half-light. As a hallmate said, you can always put up blackout curtains if you ever need to get really depressed. It was probably a mistake to clear the table. To bring some semblance of order into the apartment. I couldn't sleep that first night, convinced that the picture was luminous. It's not. I was confused by the tonal arrangement, some well-known optical illusion or base magicians' trick of indirection. The picture followed you all over the room. Seemed to. And if I'd never noticed before how light it is above the living quarters, it's maybe because I'd never looked, never stayed up all night worrying. In the end, I carried out conclusive experiments, pulled a big box over the table, buried my head inside, battened down the virtual hatches, and could see: nothing at all. Yet when I took the box off my head, the room still seemed brighter than before. Obviously, I couldn't go back in time and compare before. Not luminous then. I was mistaking it for numinous, for that, it definitely was. Drawing in my attention and just Be-ing out of the corner of my eye. Forcing itself into focus. I thought I ought to check and went down to the library the following day. You will have gathered by now that I am one of the Abstemious. It would be easy for you, of course. Checking the facts is a sacred ritual and one which depends on a total single-mindedness, a lack of any other distraction or technological support. But you knew that. It's easy to feel superior in such moments and this is where we get our strength from. So I walked to the library. Early the following morning. To find out what the hell that picture was.

The town is built on the steep hillsides of a major river, up on what we are informed (in elementary school) is in fact an eroded plateau. In other words, all the hills are around the same height, and the towns cling to the sides of the valleys, ground down by Laurentian glaciers. The riverbed goes down another couple of hundred feet, but no-one cares about that except bridge engineers, or businessmen with their own private sonars to show off on the way to a fish restaurant downstream. These days. Two hundred and fourteen feet deep. And to think I once tried to get out of a rowboat because I thought the ducks were walking on the bottom, and ducks only have short legs. That's true. But no, the cliffs carry on their plunge, down to the silt and the buried dreams, the lost suicides. So it might seem that we are nestled at the bottom of a hill, but in fact we're almost on the mountaintop. The water runs down, the snow builds up. One hard outcrop of rock, millions of years ago turned the iceflow this way rather than that, and scraped a trough. When the ice-caps melted, the streams flowed down the same courses, just faster. And the animal and human trails followed the rivers and the crests of the hills, so the roads followed the tracks of the glaciers. And the towns set up at crossroads, or a pinch in the valley, and the traffic speeds by even faster. And the birds, following the waterways. The same melody played in different keys and tempi. Even the clouds sway and part, blankets over the landscape.

I head uphill, is what I'm trying to say, back to the Devonian desert, under that historical mile of tundra, the younger dryas that wiped the slate clean. Such were my thoughts as I turned onto Franklin Street, and the former mansion that is now the library. Its chain-link fence, the uninviting parking lot where you are momentarily naked and exposed to view. Which is why you scuttle. Even if you are not actually scuttling, it's a scuttly kind of place, so you scuttle.

Inside is another story altogether. If you're lucky you might be the only person in the building. Its Dewey decimals. Today I'm after the seven-five-threes. They have some massive tomes in there. I make my own little notches in the log page. Sometimes I go back to a book I borrowed in my childhood, and discover there's only been one other reader since then. Or no-one at all. Unread books. Miles and miles of them, foxing, gathering mildew, asleep. But sometimes there might be just one or two other people lurking. Standing among the rows of shelves, leafing through this book, weighing that other. Or staggering to the reading tables with a stack of picturebooks, bowed under the load, avoiding eye contact and settling ostentatiously into the old leather seats as if there were any more purpose to their actions than that of a leaf falling off a tree, being blown to the gully and then, a year later, if it avoided becoming humus, drifting down the brook into the creek into the river and off again, mimicking those birds wintering out, or coming back with the thaw. Like some Magus in his or her château, undeterred at being a late developing teenager in a musty felt overcoat. Or tweed. Greedy for knowledge.

On this day, it was a young woman, forbidding in black, with slashes of Egyptian inspired kohl around her eyes, inexpertly applied, but off-putting nonetheless. Forty years ago I would have liked her, would have braved her bristling silences and risked a tilt of the head to attempt to decipher the titles along the spines of her carefully selected books. In those days there would have been no tattoos to help me, her palimpsest unsullied. Though she would have denied that, in the same way she would have parleyed standing next to a food truck at half-past eleven on a November night into keeping watch over the northern marches for a full year of winters. Until her lips turned indigo.

But I'd laid hands on the book I wanted. And I had been at least half-right. Encouragingly, the shot in the dark had hit an even better target than the one I had hoped to be aiming for, thus:

I did that coughing trick I remember seeing in a movie: you rip out the page you want while the cough gives a socially acceptable cover for the sound the tearing makes. Then roll up my Bosch print and stuff it up my sleeve, so as not to crease it, and trudge home in the rain pretending I hadn't violated one of my deeper principles by removing information from the public world and locking it into my own private gaol. Spread it out nicely on the un-decluttered coffee table.

It was, as you may have guessed, Hell itself. And more especially the depiction of the punishments meted out to the Seven Deadly Sins. There's an awful lot of ancillary and administrative staff down there for a relatively few sinners, which seems like a whole waste of daemonic effort and - how should I put this? - petty-mindedness on the part of the (absent, obviously) Lord, and no less a dereliction of assiduity from the haphazardly present Devils. I did not like this at all, glaring up at me in my own abode, and resolved to send it on its merry way.

I might start drinking.

But Victory and Defeat are so tightly intertwined that the one is indistinguishable from the other. It's all a trick of perspective or dependent upon the assertions of a Higher Authority, well, spare me that.

If I had hoped that by naming the Thing I could tame the Thing, I was wrong. It got no easier. In fact, attaching a concrete meaning to a formerly abstract image only made it more powerful. The room at night, when night begins at five, the fixed anti-shadows cast by the streetlights onto the wall of my room; the moving geometrical shapes thrown by the traffic. I could put up blackout curtains and dig into the gloom, but I'd just shaved and wouldn't be up to speed as a homeless extra for another day or two. Among those shadows, the Hell glowed all the stronger. From a drifted sleep, I'd come to, convinced some touchscreen was alerting me to a call, but no, just the calm patience of neg-entropy pulsing out. I covered it. I thought of what lay under the cover. Of what lay under the puzzle, its darker side. And then back into slumber. Golden Slumbers, hardly.

I woke up face down on the tiled floor. *Lastryko,* I think, cool as marble and smooth as skin. My cheek anaesthetized, and a small trickle of drool on the floor, to offset the dry scrubland of my tongue. How I came to be there, I know not. I certainly had not been drinking, neither absinthe nor Benedictine, which is also a hospital, and this now seeming like a hospital floor, looking up at the underside of the coffee table, big and ponderous, its own dark cloud. But my room has a floor of wide pine planks, not *lastryko*, or marmoreal, or whatever they market the wretched material as these days, so what is this? Symbolic perhaps? Except this is the real world, and not a dream. But then again, what's the difference, we don't remember what we dreamed, or what happened, we only recall what we remember happening, or dreaming. Which, to misquote some other South American writer, is the whole core of fantasy, one of the four conditions, if I misremember rightly, when 'dreams begin to contaminate reality'. So it little matters whether I awoke to find myself facedown on the marble, or the *terrazzo*, or the varnished planks; or whether I only half woke, and lost in the taint of the dream, imagined the symbolic surface of all those rugged individual chips embedded in concrete, like so many spermatozoid Mafiosi; and how do they make it anyway? Who did Buñuel quote wondering if Mortadella was made by blind people? Dali? Même combat. Is it solidified into buckets and then sliced into tiles? Are the chips poured onto the floor *in situ*, drowned in cement and then buffed down? How thin are the tiles? Why are they separated by thin brass runners? Hospitals and prisons and diners. Artificial granite given free rein to aesthetic theory, the colors, the shapes, the sizes. An invitation to irresponsibility. And then, not. Back on the wooden floor again, softer somehow, and lacking that famous apocryphal coolness. Sticky and all too real. One of those moments when the dream dissolves and you realize, 'Hey! I am dreaming', and that's when the trouble starts. Or in the opposite direction, life seems to be running along in its well-established groove, and then something happens to make you say, 'Hey! I must be dreaming', but then you are not. Can you fly? Do you gaze at your hand? Do you try to find a light switch to turn off the sun, or do you raise your arms to the sky and call down the wind? Other people may well, at this point, offer various levels of advice as to your waking or semi-wakeful state. Or you may get hit by a bus. What happens after that is probably decisive for your clarity. But in this case, deep into night, with my heart beating too fast, and my lungs gasping for breath, no such succor. Up above me, on the table, the image of Bosch pulsated. Or the level-crossing lights were pulsing over the room. One or the other. I looked down at the design. How would the people in that landscape know whether they were in the countryside, but just on a bad day, or in the outbuildings of hell, or Hell. How indeed do we ever tell? Well, there do seem to be an undue number of female persons eager to present their bosoms to the elements, down there, in Hell, it's a fashion statement; also, there seems to be a marked shortage of trousers in the underworld, some price fixing by cartels, no doubt; and the clincher - though again, not unheard of, just exceedingly rare, is if any of the gentlemen repeatedly clench French horns between their bared buttocks. That's the fundamental give-away.

I checked: no French horns.

I had to get rid of the painting.

It was, of course, staring me in the face all along. The pleasure principle, so oft lauded in song, or action, or inaction. Sinning by omission or commission. The stamps. I would never have kept the envelope—manila or otherwise—if they hadn't put pretty stamps on it. Six stamps along the top and down one side. More than strictly necessary. It was there, carefully flattened out in the kitchen drawer. Why I don't know don't ask me. And there, top left-hand corner, in crabbed handwriting, or written too gently on an unsteady surface, the return address (also a P.O. Box). Dilemma. The envelope enclosed within bore a different address. This made some kind of sense. Why send the puzzle back to the Company? Why not send it on to the next client? Save a double postage fee. Save two separate yet additional delivery times. Double the risk of loss and/or damage. So: where should I send it? On or back? And then again, what guarantee did I have that "back" meant "back to the Company", perhaps it meant "back to the previous client", someone just like me, or just like *fionawakefield*, at any rate. Which was the other dilemma. Does that make it a trilemma? Or a tetralemma? Possibly. In which case my solution was doubly elegant. I sent the puzzle on to the address on the front of the enclosed envelope; but I hand-wrote the same address in the top left corner as was on the top left corner of my original envelope. Are you following this? Because it's important. In other words, I took both myself and *fionawakefield* out of the loop. What could possibly go wrong? And, to bolster my confidence, or pander to my arrogance, as we will soon see, I suddenly had no problem at all looking at the rather charmingly naive Bosch painting, nor dismantling it, all numinosity bled, putting it back inside, first, its plastic Ziploc bag, then the padded manila envelope, then taking it to the old Post Office with a subtly-retro-Bauhaus-look down by the Shirt Factory, the shirt factory in which I now live, then mailing it, then fleeing the building like Pontius Pilate after that Jesus, hand-washing charade. The last piece of the puzzle, as opposed to The Puzzle, was whether to add several small but attractive stamps, or to go the full-metal-jacket administrative unemotional way with a computer printed frank. I was weak. I chose four different regular mail stamps from a series celebrating dragons. Why dragons, I have zero idea. A sop to our Chinese overlords. And off it went, to whomever, and I back to my pre-Bosch life.

But Bosch has a way of not letting go, once the cracks have appeared, so they remain, you only wonder how you didn't notice them earlier, but you didn't, and now everyone who wanted could notice them, but there's no-one around to notice them, so nobody notices them, except yourself. And you start avoiding mirrors, which are—according to that same South American writer alluded to above—abominations.

All through the night the trains run past the building. Sometimes just the rhythm of the wagons. Sometimes just the howl of the sirens, the horns drag me out of sleep almost, then let me drop gracelessly back. Or both at once, single notes, double notes, lazy melodies, or samples of the history of jazz drawn out over some mathematical grid of possibilities and probabilities, each node of the net bearing a name:

Lester Young, Coleman Hawkins, Charlie Parker, Ben Webster, Sonny Rollins...
or on the cusp of dawn, one long wail after another, dipping in, surfacing briefly then gone: Ornette Coleman, John Coltrane, Albert Ayler, Archie Shepp, Eric Dolphy...

With hindsight, this makes me feel sad that I could not justify also lauding other jazz greats, the black saints we skinny white dudes actually admire above and beyond any possible identifications or appropriation, like Thelonious Monk or Charles Mingus or Cecil Taylor, Sun Ra, Don Cherry, oh a million others exaggeratedly, probably, stuck between the airwaves, burned into the static beneath everything under this country, sailing through and blurring out, oh, and Billie Holiday, she sings sang has sung the songs the same songs The Song.

I doubt I made it past dawn, at any rate, off to the mailbox as soon as I could meaningfully pull my clothes on, and there it was, another manila envelope, but this time addressed to a surely non-existent hybrid creature, but doubtless, doubtless, aimed squarely at Yours Truly, *fionawakefield-or-currentresident,* that would be my good self. I took the package home and sulked. It's times like this one realizes the function and value—symbolic or otherwise—of a good letter opener. But who has a letter opener these days? I mean, not even I do, and if anyone were likely to, it would be me. Or some narcissist with more dollars than cents, I suppose. I'm trying to be funny now, but I was spooked, then.

In the end I used a bread knife. Tore through the wrapping and found another puzzle. What else would you expect?

But this one was teasing at my memory. No perimeter, only a fistful of center pieces, and am I naive enough to imagine this matrix could be complementary to the Hell rim? Not at all. Unless some abstract expressionist had been handed the tiller of the ship. First horses, now ships. Watch out. What I am getting at is the image was impossible to assemble, you could tell from each individual piece: random splashes and strings of unrelated color. No guide possible or proffered. But if, like myself, you can have your faculties sharpened by anger, then you will understand that the sheer necessity of pieces interlocking allows one to make a puzzle without reference to the visual sense at all. It takes a lot longer of course, but Ô the reward when the puzzle reveals its shape and meaning. White light. Free jazz.

I sat back like some sea captain in the eighteenth century poring over a badly surveyed depth chart, dubious, unproven, unreliable, revealing nothing, a map printed by imbeciles full of soundings and fathoms, signifying nothing between the mussel banks and *saumarez,* if you were hoping for any relief at all even only that simple relief of listening to yourself above the clamor of the waves, finally speaking to yourself and saying, no, no, don't get your hopes up, it's not that kind of game we're in here, together, better wait and see, drift awhile, then wait and see again. Trust yourself. But it did look remarkably like a three by two excerpt from my *lastryko* floor, and how to match that up? Blake's infinity in a grain of sand, a whole fucking beach of fine white light sand, it's in there somewhere, off you go lads, the story you were looking for, the one you wanted to tell, to comfort yourself and everyone else with, with which. But now it's back to the night sweats, all the windows of my life, up on that second floor, the red neon sign, I am inside a French film, maybe one of Godard's, where it says CIN, then ÉMA,redblue, bluered, off and on and off again, only for the observed profile, while the chattering comes in through the bounds, over, under, adjacent, through, a drizzle of prepositions. Or it could be mild food poisoning. Everything that isn't actually black making believe it is a source of light, the stained-glass windows of the slum loft, even a basement loft, they have them, you know, in Paris, in the Paris of my head, under the overpass, it could be the rain, I don't know, I can't hear it anymore.

... get a grip get a grip I tell myself in the mornings. It could be habit, some vestige of the brutish British stiff upper lip (so necessary for the shaving thereof) to resort to logic, to routine, to grooming, the razor blade dragged round the inside of the vaselined tumbler, carefully, we have all the time in the world, and then, when one is presentable, washed, spiffed and spruced up, with clean clothes, moderately well-fed and watered, any problem deemed unsurmountable the previous evening will be seen, in the cool light of day, to be another mere bagatelle, a trifle unworthy of worry, as a dog might worry a rag doll. I sent white light off with the minimum of fuss, leaving no return address, enclosing a perky seaside postcard with the legend (is that what it was?) PLEASE CANCEL SUBSCRIPTION gouged in multi-colored crayon. The picture was a hand-tinted panorama of some Catalan beach, from the early seventies, a place which no longer exists, let them trace me and track me to there, to then, even the colors are different, the tourists, for I was one, dispersed and scattered, mostly dead, I'd guess, I was just a child, and without giving too much away, it's those corners in which I intend to hide when I feel the breath of my own death too closely on my neck, they'll never find me there, the hounds, even I won't remember, I'll study forgetfulness, and sit on that beach in inclement weather, by the upturned boats, the shuttered establishments, off-season, off-piste, a million leagues away from puzzles, real or imaginary, and their pataphysical solutions. Their thens to my ifs.

We all try to blend in, to hide in plain sight, dress up as the Twig Man at Beltane, thinking sage beyond our young years (why, almost the ruddy cheeked urchin!) that merely to walk upon the very earth is such delight, and not be wrong in that assumption, but somewhere lurks a worm, and in the midst of our camouflage, we incongruously and defying all logic or prudence find ourselves—but compelled by whom other than our own selves? so strike the Judas passive voice —dancing on the table of a crowded public house with our trousers round

our ankles and our arses in the air. Though to be honest, sometimes the bohemian seems a better solution, let the stubble grow, let the shirts crease, the hair tousle and the glare turn baleful. It's the aggression I can't countenance, like the glum wrestler, I'd rather receive than throw the forearm smash. And who knows, with a wink of the eye, stagger back off the ropes to half-nelson my assailant before dropkicking the bastard into next week. Me and Les Kellett. So much for non-violence.
Try telling that to Kali, All-Compassionate-Blueskinned-Mother-Goddess-of-Chaos-and-Destruction.
Forewarned is four-armed.

Put another way, I opened my big mouth again. The nervous tic gave me away. I had given myself away by even condescending to play their game. I wrote back. Polite yet full of my own kind of compassion (so unlike that of dearest Kali) I had as good as sent my own personal GPS co-ordinates to the gang of wingèd assassins peppered throughout my past. The cost of cowardices piled up like pyramids of skulls, the jawbone-scythes toothless and useless. The flying monkeys were on their way. Yet someone, or some consortium of self-congratulatory, glib, bearded types, had put themselves out to the extent of finding an apposite reply, a manner of hurting me deeper by the appropriacy of their co-written, spitballed rejoinder: a boastful 1936 souvenir chromolithograph from the Alcázar in Toledo, first redoubt of the Falange. Which therefore somewhat trumped my facetious tourist bauble from Peñíscola. Trumped for seriousness. And its own legend in a similar mood.

"Just as one cannot invite oneself, nor can one disinvite oneself."

Duly noted. I decided to put an end to this futile correspondence and stare a human being in the face. That return address. It was less than one hundred miles away.

Everything in its right place. A small manufacturing town in the finger lakes. Nothing much happens there. Things get stored. There isn't even a bus, or a train anymore. Twice a week. You can hitch, or hire an üBER, and do a lot of waiting around. But you'll get there. The empty main street an uneasy hybrid of fifties style boarded former businesses and lame-ass high concept storefronts. Cupcakes. Artisanal teas. Hand-tooled leather goods. Native American blankets just not native from round here as the natives from round here aren't from round here, they come from Europe mostly and Asia a few and Africa but who's asking them? they didn't even come under their own steam. There's a water cycle, a nitrogen cycle, a carbon cycle, but did you know there's also a rock cycle? igneous, sedimentary metamorphic *da capo al fine*, and there's definitely a people cycle, watch! here they come ouch! there they go. So, the town's empty, mostly, been bought as a toy for the feckless children of the ruthless. And the deserted manufactories, partially renovated by well-meaning oafs convinced that there's a market somewhere for giant state-of-the-art hand-carved ultra-fi wooden speakers and/or mangrove root lampshades, I kid you not. The other end of the god-awful end-of-America road is entirely taken up with law enforcement and county administration. There's a buzz during the weeks, but at weekends or on holy days even a tumbleweed would get lonesome. I don't need a GPS, the addresses are still ordered according to a logic I can understand, numbers, points of the compass, legible family names (Smith, Jones) or locations (East does meet West here, down with Robert Johnson at the crossroads) or functional (Main, Division, Water, Partition).

That de Chirico day. No-one but no-one on the streets. The plate glass windows dulled, concert flyers from three years ago still pasted up in the corners. Inside, worktables and plastic chairs, off in the depths, the fade under sodium lamps, a double door. I'm asked in, once I explain my dumb mission, tracking down the mail order firm. Ah, he says, that'll be in back, and he walks me in back, which I assume is another large room, maybe Manhattan style, but no... this room beyond the doors goes back far, far, too far. Brick archways in a dizzying perspective and a second double door at the end. I had walked all around the building before examining the frontage and the block just isn't that deep, not half, and it backs onto a creek anyway. I look out of the window, and we're already two stories high. It's night out there. It's all emptiness. The walls and ducting unfinished, out with the old, in with the new. Every ten feet, over every archway, a black disc, a flashing red light, a pinprick. Motion detectors, don't worry, he says. They have numbers on them in LED. I see clearly sixty-five, sixty-four, sixty-three...as we walk down. What's through that door? I ask. Oh, he says, you should see that. So we see that. The doors open onto a glass walled bridge leading up to the factory on the creek, over the back road, and that building is twice as big as the one out front, the whole built on a steeply dropping off slope to the wharf. And whoever used to operate from here, years ago, no longer does so. The hardware store has gone but the micro-brewery hasn't hopped up yet. Numbers numbers, *mene mene tekel upharsin*. So I took the bus back to the train and the train back towards home then a bus even closer then I walked and I did not take the shortest route, once again calling attention to myself and making the children point at me. When I say children I don't mean children, I mean the teenage and older boys who stand idle on streetcorners, in gaggles and huddles, but I call them children rather than thugs because a) they are still very young even though they consider themselves, with respect, as old and wise as the hills, and b) I have no evidence that they actually commit thuggery, when even the older local hooligans don't bother me though I understand they have their own good reasons to stand where I want to stand, under the thruway flyover in the dark, with the tardy cats aloof and escaped supermarket trolleys reclining to take the weight of the world off their wheels. But that's not how it happened.

I wasn't alone. The town wasn't by the finger lakes, it was just north of the Catskill mountains, which are mountains even if they can fool you, under certain lights, into suspecting they might only be hills. But Main Street is deserted, almost. A couple of isolated and outlying young black men make friendly noises in shop doorways, and this, the abandoned hardware store, looking as though some activity had finally happened, in a town center abandoned these fifteen years now. The cinema was still open, the marquee aflame, just a few doors down, though the last show was already underway and the lights still civilizing half the block. Then the vast former haberdashery store, now full of folding white tables and crowded—how can this town crowd anything?—with boy-men in shorts and hoodies playing magic cards and other Hex Enduction boardgames. Then, closer than that, a sliver of the same space leased out to a hipster bar, the Hi-Lo, bringing not only a Taste o'Bushwick, but a busload of its inhabitants up to the country to sip their cocktails and watch DVDs of German *Neue Welle* films while Thurston Moore lookalikes play their ambient industrial on detuned guitars. Then the duskroom. Two massive, I use the word judiciously, massive cubic cabinets with a cone carved into their fronts, meticulously, with craft, dare I say unreservedly with love? ring after ring, as if a tree had been hollowed out in the form of a funnel. I peer inside and a curly haired young man leaps over and asks if he can help me. He can. I notice I am in one of those rare liminal situations not merely straddling an actual lintel, but also the twilight state between dream and wakefulness, that oneiric reality I was bothering you about up there, as contrasted with the lucid dream of the holy grail, state so belovèd of mushroom gatherers micro-dosing their way back to normality instead of lying in the gutter looking up at the moon like the rest of us. The street is wet with rain. No-one, now no-one at all is visible. Cars are parked, but no traffic on the street in either direction. No vehicle crosses the line. The boot is on the other vampire hunting foot, for they have asked me inside, a classic gambit to disorient, I suspect, wait, amn't I supposed to invite you in? Or the contrary? The traffic lights drift through their cycle unobserved. Inside the room, the young man explains what the constructions are: solid wood stereo speakers he hand-carved himself. It's what he does for a living now. He's lurking in his unlit shopfront at night because it's so quiet, he can calibrate the room. That's when I notice that what I'd taken for construction stands dotted about the room all have microphones fitted. The loose stacks of ceiling panels, or so I thought, turn out to be acoustic tiles that the young man is placing to kill echoes and break standing waves. Would I like to listen? Yes, I imagine I would. He spins his laptop around and keys me into his Spotify account. I could listen to anything. I choose Robert Wyatt's version of 'Shipbuilding', so I can check the clarity

of the opening cymbals. I can say I have never heard a sound so clear, so centered, and so all-enveloping. Then he plays me some mushy New Age jazz which, despite its evident and palpable spatialization still sounds to me like peplum, something a spatially aware infant gymnast might have vomited out during a particularly energetic double-backflip-with-triple-pike, difficulty seven-point-five, and invited one to rechew or mop up. I guess I am a content man, when all is said and done. (That's stress on the first syllable: what it's about; not stress on the second syllable: basically happy.) That's when he invited me into the back and the real world slipped away. Some trick of perspective stretched the unlit backroom to infinity, and that door leading to the glass bridge, it's real I swear, you can stand in the middle and see half the town, the black waters of the creek and the wholly empty warehouse that the architects' impression has peopled with the hip, the happy and the wholesome. Does our world need more hand-cast pots? I felt sorry for the young man. He didn't tell me his full name, I knew straight away that was because he thought I'd recognize it, but he misoverestimates me. I found out later on, and I'd never heard of him or his cleanly acquired billions. Still, twenty-eight is probably not a mentally healthy age at which to retire. Your soul will swell up like bread with too much yeast, tending to the ergot. If you ask me. And what's a mentally healthy age anyway, a healthy mental age, divided by a hundred and expressed as a percentage?
One-oh-three.

So, when I got back home, calmed by the sudden showers, all I had was the certainty that whoever was responsible for mailing out the jigsaw fragments and their Chinese fortune cookie mottos no longer had any connection with the vast, rambling and entirely dubious warehouse/workshop to the north. A dead end, a red heron, while the blue herons fly.

The rest is true.

Imagine my surprise, then, a week later, when an official looking-envelope (the kind with a translucent window at the lower right) arrived a wolf disguised as a mere bill. Inside the envelope, a grayscale rendition of a scanned photo of myself looking pensive—an answer to the question "how do you photograph 'listening'?" which was indeed a photograph of myself listening to the music on the vast wooden speakers. I'd let my defenses down, obviously, a lesson for thought controllers everywhere: crank up the volume and make it sound nice and clear.

> [I should interject here that an event occurred which gave me pause for thought, but a little context is required. I may have given the impression up above that I am some kind of sociopath, living in half-decayed, lo-rent accommodation and ekeing out what might be assumed to be what remain of my days hiding from the light and garnering nourishment only from some aural parallel photosynthesis that is powered by the sound of rain on a corrugated tin roof. Well, no. I'm relatively—not to say depressingly—normal psychically, or not, and am free, when not otherwise engaged, to do whatsoe'er I will. That may indeed involve lying under my bed listening to the weather, or waiting until there are storms to clear the streets before going out, but not always.]

Home had changed. I had only been away for a single day—not even overnight—but the room had lost all of its lustre. The sunlight too bright, casting shadows and preventing the objects from settling in their rightful places, in their own softness. The kind of morning light that makes your hands appear all fingernails, and pulls all the sounds apart until they grow edges. What happens when you know what you should be doing but you are not doing it. To be honest, most people spend most of their lives in that state. So, I can't blame home, or that temporary building that was standing in for home. It was nice in a way, as many of my temporary stand-ins have been. That airy apartment on the top floor in Seattle; the triangular room at the point of the horsemeat restaurant, by its red neon sign in the Fifteenth Arrondissement of Paris, France, by the old abattoirs and the famous leavened bread bakery; the apartment on the top floor of Mme. Blavatsky's building, which bore gold mosaic swastikas (pre-Hitler) on the frontage; my rundown flat in Russafa in Valencia, all smoky tiles and shutters; even that duplex bolthole in the Rondout with the cathedral window and the giant water rats running through the kitchen at night. Not their fault. I've lived in twenty-nine different houses with nineteen different people and it was never their fault.

It's that satisfying thud we are cautioned to expect and demand: that what happens next is both inevitable yet unexpected. Then we can cut through the crap and abandon all of those carefully constructed positions and ripostes, the wit so brief as to be non-existent, a Buster Keaton so adept at cutting to the chase that the entire film is only chase.

I needed to go somewhere, out of the house, to solve this mystery, the whats and the wheres. And I only had one address untapped: where I had been sending everything on to. I went to bed early, to enable me to get up ever so much earlier the following morning, and carry out that plan. I put on my old Tweed overcoat, my wire-rimmed reading spectacles, and my strong walking shoes, thus girding my loins for the most important day. I too left no forwarding address.

As I closed the door behind me, careful not to lock it, so that the next tenant could enter with minimal fuss, I could not but notice the small plastic bag on the threshold, In it, innocent of annotation, one single puzzle piece: both sides black, unmarked. No matter. Into my pocket, and I, on to the train.

When I reached the city. When I found my way. When I missed a bus. When I had a sandwich. When I walked along. When I. When I. and Then I. Agency. Found the address. Some fraction of Brooklyn. A neighborhood that I for one ignored the appellation of. Someone somewhere would be making a buck off of it. East-northwest midtown sub-Williamsburg perhaps? Not promising. No stores. Few houses, I always used to think that communities accreted round churches, rivers, bridges, fords, crossroads and immutable trees. Oaks, probably. But no. No longer. Just a line of an architect's Rotring Isograph, a slip of the pen that creates or condemns square miles here, hectares there. Half blocks and *manzanas*. Get there first, read about it when it's too late. Turn up in Barcelona in 1986. ¿Where is La Pasionaria? Hit Paris, but miss Hemingway. Then, Berlin. Senseless.

So this streetlet has one low building bending into a triangle. The southern half is a pickle bottling factory. And the only other doorway leads into an L-shaped space with high ceilings up to the skylit roof. No-one outside, no sign, no bouncers or guards. So I go inside.

Oh, but inside, a hundred people around dozens of tables. Sofas and low tables. I am out of place here. The people too various and young. Too absorbed in what they are doing, and what are they doing? On each table, a work-in-progress jigsaw puzzle. Will I find *currentresident* in here? Where is *fionawakefield*? No-one looks up, no-one pauses. There are empty seats. Some people mill around, others stand thoughtful, examining the pieces set before them. Occasionally, a piece is moved and slotted into the design. Perhaps, though, I have been here before, perhaps I've always been here, like everyone else sitting around tables poring over their own incompleteness, while I stand, overcoated, clutching my own missing piece in my hand, knowing that it fits in somewhere, maybe more than one place, because everything fits in somewhere, it's a law of the galaxy, not infinite or even near infinite, what the Scientists call a Very Big Number, but far from statistical magicks and skullduggery, that there is a fit somewhere, unless like that single apocryphal monkey among all the other monkeys suddenly becoming self-aware up a lonely tree in a jungle somewhere somewhen, only to realize that it's the only one, and there'll be no comeback to that until evolution has woken up, no furry partner to exchange a caress with, to pick the nits off, so back to sleep lonely monkey, it's going to stay cold cold cold, it's not time yet; or that mythical alien civilization '*x*' light years away that runs its course for tens of thousands of years and develops space travel, see I told you it was science fiction, and reaches out to that other civilization '*x*' light years away, or to us, striving for our own tens of thousands of years of culture, only it's not the same tens of thousands of years, they are a million years apart and anyway, it's not ten light years, but ten million light years, oh still in our neighborhood I hear you say, same side of the Great Attractor, so ne'er the twain shall meet, our windows of opportunity looking out onto different universes, practically, in different directions, so the question is wrong from the get go, are we not alone? Yes, we are, but why look so far? Here in the café, all those shuttered windows, all those noughts after the decimal point of zero zero zero zero etcetera, then a single 'one'; or added to the end in the probability fraction one in another lonely 'one', followed by zero zero zero zero zeros etcetera—its reciprocal—all wiped away by the here and now, be here now, well here I am.

He sat at the single remaining empty table and ordered a coffee.

Coda.

Coming out of the city at midnight, the tunnels run off into the dark in every direction, the lights closer, then suddenly far across vast galleries. Sometimes I think I glimpse people running, but that can't be right. Then the lights get further away, the galleries deeper, still subterranean, until the black rushes from you apace, and snakes off across the river, and you know you are above ground again, sudden night, because light has not come here yet, in Haarlem or Broncks, Tubby Hook, Spuyten Duyvil, under the surrealistic towers and high arched bridges that lattice the boroughs together like Delvaux would have, given the chance, then suburbs, the river wider now, to the left, the lights spaced rhythmically, night above, and the sound of the wheels danang-kanang, danang-kanang, only this time it's not a freight train pulling past, it's your heart and you are inside.

the one about the icebergs

i HAVE BEEN SELLING my blood for quite some time now, it's a thing to do, at first, it's barely worth the effort, but if you stick it out and follow the rules, it can be a nice little earner, in time, and yes, of course, accidents do happen, but generally it's not the worst way of supplementing your income, and then again, not all accidents are unhappy ones

it was spring turning summer, this i remember, for a few days in a line everything breathed possibility, you'd wake up a-morning in the cool, bright air, go out into the streets without a jacket, among the girls in dresses, air on the upper arm, and that chill just as the sun goes down, not even enough thirst to discomfort you, not in these maydays yet, i stroll from sidewalk to sidewalk, barrio to barrio, doing nothing but step and breathe, some musics in my head, some people i might catch up with, when it's dark again, when the sky turns blue and the windows yellow, the lights zigzag black on the river, but everyone's still about

the best thing about the blood deal is that they give you cash in hand as well as all the water you can drink, and it's the good stuff, too, of course, they search you on the way out, i suppose some of their clients abuse their privileges, but not me, no sir, maybe it's not my focused clarity then, maybe i am a little light in the head as i float through the city, who would notice?

i walk ahead and my clothes float at the same speed, but on a different layer, you can hardly tell, if you didn't know, but some drift through the air, others wave in water like weeds, and the sneakers step/stop in a weird dance like in a silent film in one of those retro cafés, i'm naked inside all of that, in a suit of oxygen, blood-thinned, my retinas stretched out over my face in the breeze, seeing the wind in 360° until the crosswalk, when i let all the momentum and gravity catch up with itself, all the layers collide, to you it looks as though i am waiting for the lights to change, but no, look closer, i am half an inch above the ground, and not even in love, not this day, because today i found an apartment

of course i am thirsty, because with the best will in the world, no hospice is going to let you just guzzle away pint after pint, they have to think about their bottom line, but i never do manage to hold down the euphoria when i leave the building with coin in my pocket, fluid replenished, and the plasma topping itself up with each step, the world is mine and on i walk for giddy miles until the tongue dries to remind me to sit in the shade, to lie a little, until i get moved on, not high summer yet, you know how that can kill, navigating from the one free bathroom to the next, the air-conditioned passages from marble lobby to service corridor, to fire exit, then criss-cross the block to stay out of the baleful sun, keep on the shady side, duck into maintenance closets if you think the guards are on to you, keep checking that the sweat on your arms is still cool it wasn't always like this in the city, the old folks will tell you it used to be even worse, but then, in the same anecdote, they'll tell you how you could eat a good meal, not the kind of pulp they serve you these days, for three dollars and change, and their rent was a hundred a month, all cheap and cheerful, everything in its right place, everyone in their own shoes, and the neighbors smiled at you, didn't matter where you came from, or what language you spoke, we're all human, right?

admitting it was even worse then, then, still gets you in a bind because people then used to have jobs, even the unemployed had a job that they weren't doing or weren't allowed to do, people shared apartments, and not just married folks or solid couples, friends did it too, or college room-mates, workers, the whole island near sank under the weight of fifteen million people in three million rooms, and you can bet your last penny that the place was striped top to bottom according to the color and odor of the occupants' skins, and their distance from the upper airs

i run through this city like a thread, i see myself that way, every day, drawing it through streets, alleys, into office buildings, cafés, stores, finding out the back exits, the bathrooms that aren't locked and guarded, the few forgotten water points—how few, how totally forgotten—and out again onto the next block, the other backstreet, just like you do, if that's what you do, your warp, my weft, weaving the city together, my thread is red

another thing that annoys me about 'timers is how they always go on about their bijoux apartment or their once-in-a-lifetime loft space as if that was anything other than describing a streetcorner or a park bench, that they used to have to lock themselves up inside every night and make their room dark, makes me laugh, so what did they do to keep moving? everybody knows that if you never move you get sick, that it's sitting and lying down that killed all the ancient civilizations such as the mayans, the pilgrims, the turks, and that if you or i nap more than a couple of hours, better call the medics because we're already on the way out, how did they ever get anything done sleeping all the time?

i never get over the view when i go up onto the roof, past the remaining projects, broken teeth, as in former days out to sea, you could see it if you knew where to look, but now no question, five miles offshore, standing as tall as manhattan heights, the icebergs, night factories, cloud *maquiladores*, sublimating steam, lit up day night day night, you think it must be snow-capped mountains but no, it's just a little sliver of tundra calved off and harvested, still the people remain the great unwashed

that one time i went out, in the chumbucket boat from sheepshead bay, i don't know how or why i said yes, thought it would be educational, i expect, which it certainly was in the dawn fog, or would have been, if we'd been the only citizens out there in shaky leaky boats piloted by speed freaks, but there must have been dozens of us, veering in and out of the cool mists, you'd hear them first, the music they were blasting, and i kept wondering why don't they just listen to the winds? no-one can really see us so why make it easy for them to hear us, that's the deathwish that k talks about i suppose, but i don't have a deathwish and i was getting jumpy despite all the beauty, i always saw the beauty which on the one hand saved me on the other damned me, i mean i'd be the one on the stairway to hell stopping to admire the stalactites and getting hooked by the dæmons, or the store detectives, if I was shoplifting, or redistributing wealth, as k calls it, i'd get those days where i just knew i was invisible, no-one could see me, not even security cameras, and i could rip out and slit and pop off all the anti-thefts with a whirl of the body, like a flamenco dancer, or *sevillanas,* picking the apple, a small hex wrench with a little fork on the end, and a magnet, that takes care of most of the tags, drop it in someone's pocket and stroll out of the back entrance, which would make it an exit, right? but here on the ocean it was a different game, a different scale, for a beginning, the guards were all armed with shoot-to-kill orders, but then again, they were up on the ice plateaux, far far above, and had to run all over, careless of what was real ice, what flimsy cosmetic border and what other pure augmentation, a solid wall to fall through with that ô of surprise on your face, but of course, taking care not to slide and slip off the edges, and if you were fast, and if you didn't get shot at right away, you could count on thirty seconds or so before anyone spotted you or took any action, now admittedly it takes even a half awake crew nearly half an hour to slice off a decent sized chunk, so the tactic would be to pull alongside the wall of ice, hack into it, leave a marker, then zoom off back into the fogs, only returning to pick up the work once we'd made sure there was no-one taking aim at us, which as i say, the blaring music from our coævals did not facilitate, but haha then again, they'd be the ones taking the bullets like willing drunken decoy ducks, so, we'd get a few blocks snagged and back out, and call that a good sunday's work, and stuff a chunk of canada into your personal backpack on top of the wages, take it to the café, dump it onto the counter, running and dripping onto the parquet floor, kick back and smile, and hey it's still morning

doing something, wanting to do something, not being able to do something, these are the pivots of my life and health, that I can, that i can't, that i desire, that i lack desire, that i cannot, that i nevertheless do, and i was thinking about music, about silence, about connecting thinking back with the body, the body we lost, though it's always right there, just beside us, when it should be around us, that we are in it, thus music, to tie the loose ends, with rhythm

that was a long night, many nights in truth but i lost track, lost time, lost space, when i had all but resigned myself, why resigned? triumphantly only to look forward, ahead, then get tied up looking back over my shoulder, to make sense of it all, to line up the shifting constellations, not this causing that, but all these things occurring together, as events move past each other and we call that a thing, it didn't grow, it didn't fade, the separate things moved past each other and continued their trajectories then were gone

i cannot deny that what is happening to me is sapping my mind there's no reason why it should but the sweating the lack of sleep the sharp pains and my agitated wandering betray the damage otherwise how could I have misplaced so many days in my head? how could i have all these gaps like bad dreams or not exactly empty dreams gliding through empty streets the streets are never empty day or night empty head and then wake up back here eventually in an empty room alone and aching

ô sheepshead bay one of the 'timers told me how it used to be in the good old not so good old days when everyone came from there and thence shall everyone return like blessèd bethlehem

sometimes when i get sick and just weak like this i feel i should visit r up in the high hundreds, he's got a pet, i know that doesn't sound likely but it's true and sometimes he'll let you come in and pet his pet, it's called flossy which is his little joke, as it's not flossy at all but in a way maybe it is because you can cuddle up and stroke it and it seems to understand, the way i guess animals all do or did or can, but so strongly, what is ailing you and just soothe everything away and not like sleep or being out of it, it just all starts to feel better and warm and it doesn't matter any more, but r is a bit of a tricky customer with his delicate *quid pro quo* all the time and i have to get a little stronger first or i'll just expire outside his door, which isn't good for anyone's business, no, so, wrap up, drink water, stay home

i thought i was getting used to the treatments but i had no idea, it's unfair how they have all the knowledge and all the time, all you do as they say is turn up, eat a meal and drink some water then go back home, unless you become one of their favorites which, naturally, i did, in which case they start asking you back more often and offering you a sleepover and better food and more water, and of course more money, so what do you want? you do first you go with your friends, how else would you know where to go, an endless circle or chain of bad faith friendships dragging the unwary after the half aware, maybe they got paid for recruitment, i never recruited anyone so i wouldn't know, but there I was and soon you get selected and separated from your so called friends, quite deliberately so you can't compare notes i suppose and but then you make new friends but again that's ok too from their point of view because you can't or don't meet outside, unless you do, which is how i started to understand the whole system

yes the food is better when you sleep over but haha there's a catch which i think someone must be laughing all the way at our sick smiles and innocent nodding heads, you come in for the first sleepover and the meal is so dull, just puréed vegetables and gravy and pure water well I'm not knocking that and then you go to bed in a very simple single room, i should have been warned by the tiled floors who puts tiled floors in a bedroom, but ô you just drop right off to sleep like diving into a warm lake and then wake up in agony of stomach cramps in the middle of the night, soiling the sheets, voiding every which way and straining the diaphragm, tiled floors suddenly make some kind of sense, but even then i didn't put two and two together, no, not until the breakfast when everyone sat there looking all delicate and wan, circles under their eyes and yes surely some of that nice pap would be just the thing, a nice porridge of sawdust and oatmilk, and so it was, but that day the food was out of this world and everyone had such an appetite and by the time evening came we were all pretty steady on our feet again, and ravenous to have actual warmed-over victuals and fresh fruit in the evening but they made us take our morning stool onto a white enameled metal plate, and took the plates away looking very pleased, as i think i said it was a strange job, defecating for science and after three days of that you could go home again, or onto the streets, or wherever you could hide from the weather and crowds and vermin until the next time which had to be at least two weeks later, to let you recuperate

as if those persons could just be sloughed off and left there in the past quite naturally without pain or confrontation and then related to ideally without possibilities of contradiction by new facts new falls new ideas or the random generation of change through time

it gets exhausting

now i've got more money than you can shake a fist at, and despite the feeling that I am somehow being hollowed out, i am arguably in the best shape ever, mostly down to the apartment, i'd imagined such things, but you never, you know, never, heard about this kind of thing, and i have not been telling anyone a breath about it either, you know a betrayal is just a secret you only told to one person, so

i went back into that lobby, the cool one, intending to slide out of the back side door, but again, they'd persuaded one of the big guys from up-up to come down and look around the place so i couldn't just sneak in, it's a not a dance i could have learned or remembered either, into the side door why was it open not locked and up a deafening metal staircase, the big mister up-up right on my tail moving rather gracefully for a stout fellow, some enhancement going on there, obviously, but i can leap a decent flight myself when pushed to it, and somehow, even with my new hollowed bird bones, i had the strength to leap off onto the ledge and we stood there in great stalemate, he couldn't reach me and i couldn't go back, i'd never have got a run-up, and it was a miracle i landed right on the ledge not cannoned off the wall and down the flights to the bottom, but there you go, what is, is

the ledge tapered toward a steel column, so i just started that shuffle, while mister up-up watched me and muttered something into his sleeve, i know i shouldn't have waved as i slid behind the column, but it seemed a nice gesture, hoped i wouldn't meet him again, because people can carry grudges you know and probably paranoid, think it was something about him not about me, but there i was sidestepping slowly to my left into the crevice behind the column, and hoping also that this didn't end up being an ever thinning wedge, where I'd just get stuck and rot and be found by some dusty archaeologist in a million years and they'd speculate why the inhabitants put slices of thin dried meat into their walls, no, i'd be picked clean æons before that, just some wedged bones in a pile of dust, but no, there really was a passage there, if you didn't panic or mind your ribs being snapped, and as i may have said i once got used to all that, then the walls got half a breath wider, and i shuffled sideways a step two three and soon i was in a gap between two walls, going high as high, but i could move between them, see the mold markings on the concrete, between two buildings, but not in the dark, a low slanted light filtering through and then, out i came into a small and perfectly cubical room, wide enough that i could stretch out without touching any walls, but a pit, nonetheless, and sign of life, a metal ladder going straight up overhead, and so of course i climb and come out in an enormous room, or more accurately a cavern hacked out of the side of two buildings, & up above, led to by an extension of the ladder, is a long thin strip of glassbrick roof, the whole place has no purpose, or maybe it did but no-one bothered to cut a doorway, well i would cut a doorway, but for now the problem was not how to get in, it was how to get out, unless i could learn quickly how to get nourishment from concrete dust

i know it wasn't really a fever, but the fever broke last night, woke up in the cold dawn thinking of toni, a girl i grew up with, gone now, her laughter, swimming between each other's legs in the pool, laughing, in the sunshine, but she was accident prone, then she joined the army and went to fight, or to stand in the desert and watch the sands, then she had a horse fall on her and broke her hip, and then and then and then, she got sick and died, or did she have another one of her many accidents, i stop knowing and switch to hearsay, all of that woke up with me in one concentrated drop, toni, and how her entire life scarce left a single ripple, there are others of course, but today it's toni. Antonia

nobody should let themselves be terrorized by a city skyline, but it happens, when you wake up after one of those nights, hollowed out with a spoon, cold ground on colder skin, as if the whole world is frozen caught crossways in the cruel sun lit from above by the floor of the upstairs ledge looking down

it wasn't a dream, i want to stress that, this happened, it's not a huge thing, or perhaps it is a huge thing, a hinge of the universe, early morning out on that beach, the sun coming horizontally, a cold breeze, really night had just burned off, sitting on the fine pebbles, put my head between my knees and look down, bright light, there, between my feet, all the tiny rock fragments, no bigger than the nail of my little finger, a small stone is quivering, rocking back and forth incredibly fast, stones don't do that, but as i watch i see that this rock does, it vibrates, twitches like the innards of a swiss pocket-watch, and if one, then all of them, on a beach of a billion billion tiny pebbles, all vibrating, faster or slower, to the wind, rocking back and swinging forward again, held in an equilibrium of motion, i watch for at least five minutes, i'm not going nowhere, and the little rock isn't neither, i know it is i, in some kind of certain way, that we am, trembling on the beach, dead and alive, same thing, then i stand up, the sands shift, the stone falls and stops moving, ah well, but i know it's still wound like a spring, everything is, tensed and waiting to burst apart, i turn and trudge back up the beach, thinking of blood, bone, and light

what i said about constellations, as k said to m, we get so worked up about things that don't exist, and we pass by simple things that underpin our entire lives, there are no constellations, just frozen patterns seen from where we are, invisible and non-existent from anywhere else, yes, m said, but if all of these constellations are only visible from exactly where we are and nowhere else in the universe, doesn't that mean we are in a very special place?

i've been thinking about the hat-man for some reason, i never knew him or his real name or anything about him except he never seemed to carry money, but he was always scheming, and wore very expensive cowboy hats, so something wrong there, i should have guessed, sleeping on c's floor for no rent, i mean, who pays rent anyway? but he got some perverse pleasure out of it, always talked about it like he'd figured out the secret of the universe, bumming off c for some floorspace, and she too wrapped up in her own little best of all possible worlds to see what was going on, he'd giggle, keep his overheads down, it was kinda ugly considering c was pulling three jobs and doing the community library work, while he just sat around and got out of his face, but i digress, i never liked him, hat-man, but i didn't have to, i barely knew c really, until that day when i heard and it made so much sense, but not the worst, which i will get to, trust me, that he'd been found out in the street at night, unable to walk and blood in a pool around his feet, sitting on the steps saying, lordy, lordy and uh-oh, like some dumb kid who's been caught stealing cookies, then getting gently taken away, but only later did it come out about the messican guy who'd locked him out of his own house and called the cops, so c had been living like a parallel secret life, but good secrets, not bad ones that most people would hide, good ones in case we thought she was soft, or rich, i mean she had an actual apartment, didn't she, while we... but i had told her it wasn't normal with the hat-man, that she shouldn't just let him stay there, he'd get ideas, and she'd laugh and say what? he's like a big kid, it's not like that, but i could see it was like that, at least i assumed so and that's a hard place, you can't even speak about it, can you? how she'd make no concessions to his feelings, why should she? they weren't any kind of couple, and she didn't have time for guys anyway, or girls either, but my friend j said, and some people mind his way with language and say he's crude, and don't pay any more attention, but i appreciate his bluntness, and to be truthful what he's talking about is way more crude than his what words describe, sure, he says, but she got that fine body, and hat-man gonna look and brood in the spirals of his tiny brain, and grow all cozy in his assumptions and let them fester, but that's not the worst, and i'm not one out for retribution, i don't believe in that, but what a world, eh? so one night he's sitting there and must have been wanting something but doesn't get it not even an acknowledgement, like j says any time a guy spends half his time mooning up at a girl, he really wants to run his clammy hands all over her, and starts to hate her when she keeps blanking him, you better believe it, and then she walks past him again, like he's invisible, and it's enough for him to see her so close and so out of reach so he goes into the kitchen and gets a knife and starts stabbing at her, until he gets bored or changes his mind, like he's found some better nature suddenly, maybe try a different tack, so he goes out into the street waving the knife and starts yelling at passers-by and this big messican guy comes up to him, and you'd think hat-man would be frightened, being just a poor defenseless little white boy in the big, scary city, but no, and the big messican guy, why we say messican automatically anyway? and bug them rotten with all that sinko de mayo crap, i don't know, just as likely be salvadorean round there but alright, shorthand, this guy just sidles around him and gets to the street grille and slams the door shut and calls the cops, hat-man sits on the stoop and sticks the knife in and out of his own leg, to sort of punish himself, to be seen to be punishing himself, and by the time the cops get there half an hour later c is dead, all bled out, and he hands them the knife and meekly goes off with them, that's when he makes the all-guys-together joke so well-reported at the time, 'uh-oh, there goes my free rent', i don't think anyone laughed, so yes we were all shocked and upset, which is an achievement in itself, and we even did one of those things-that-you-do and had a wake, and raised a few dollars for a memorial plaque at the library, like twenty bucks or something, and her parents came down and really who has parents who would come down? and the father grabbed j's arm, thinking he was the most manly one around, if he only knew, and the mother said, kurt sings the national anthem at stealers' field, and then the old man started singing ô say can you see in a quivery voice and everyone else just shuts up dead, it was grief skidding into madness right before our ears, which was just flat out, old-fashioned sad, because there was nothing we could do for either of them, they looked so damned helpless hugging each other and staring off into the sky, then sniffing and snuffling in the silence, i said, you have a lovely voice, which he certainly did not, but good luck to him even getting through a single verse of the song, if that made him feel any better, and they shuffled off back into their weird little lives, and then there was just more nothing, c wasn't there anymore and no-one had ever hung out with hat-man on his own so we had no particular idea about him, until i heard he'd been taken to some upcountry rehab, and there was something about his medication, but the cops knew nothing, and then we knew nothing and what was his real name anyway? and nothing in the news and nothing on the grapevine, just nothing at all, and it all just blew over, but a couple of years later, and i don't know if this is actually true, by one of those long chains you can never trace back, we are sitting in a subway car and there's a guy with one of those same hats gets on, and j says to me, oh, did you hear about hat-man? so i say no, and j says, yes, i heard he got off because his family has a lot of clout, he said clout, and they said the boy was ill, and he didn't mean it, so they put him in a nice hospital for a while, and now he's ok, and getting better, and doing painting again, well i never knew him do anything at all never mind painting, and this is the worst thing, as i said before, that we heard word of him, which sounds plausible, but i don't know, and that he is very sorry about what happened, which i suppose must have come through his parents, but now all he wants to do is put it all behind him and concentrate on his art, which is the worst thing of all, it all just slipped away, and i remember back when i heard, that she was twenty-six and he was twenty-nine, that's not right i said, they were the same age, until i realized, yes, they used to be, but her numbers stopped and his did not, and j just coughed in that way of his, like a short, quiet hyena bark, and said aw well, she gets a plastic plaque on the wall of a kids' library, so that's all right, and i didn't have the heart to tell him the library closed anyway and now it's just a storefront that sells cupcakes

i want to tell you about gowanus, it's the place that i know and they say it's rough but it's not, just there are one or two rough people live here, but they do the rough things to each other, it's not rough for the rest of us, like everything else it started as a dump, but even the worst dump has its edges, the thousands, the tens of thousands of containers dumped there, at first one atop the other, but then rotted, rusted out, fallen apart until a quick spar here, a hidden weld there and slowly the stacks become a maze, a 3D maze more than a mile long, snaking down to the old riverbed, anything and everything, and when you push two containers apart you make a third space between, by the side, and put a roof on that, a corridor, really, throw old clothes on the ground, or on the container below, or a container across above and so on and so forth, the rats go this way, the people go that and the whole resonates with the pulse, the rhythm, the stench and the hammering

tonight i woke up in the dark, cold and clammy, heart beating madly from some dream of anxiety and hiding, what is this, why the bile, the confusion, nothing is happening, but i remember being told this happens when they feed you meat, it was meat for sure, what kind or why i don't know, everything seemed so perfect and clean, it looks clean but then this happens, panting like a hunted animal, fresh, they said, everything is fresh, and interesting to learn that fear can migrate through their death panics into their still living flesh and thus into your blood into your dreams

it's a sign that your body is ready, they said, when it starts to reject anything but the best, the most pure, who decides that i thought, well, the same people that decide everything, i can hear coming back, i should grow up sometimes, i never liked to say them even though sometimes, sadly we have to conclude that there is a them, even if they are all chopped up, separated and in fragments, like the rest of us, small mercies

it passes

the next day, cold on the floor, you can see now how things evolve on their ownsome, little piles of clothes, it's not summer forever, all of it brought in a piece at a time, a plank at a time and balanced up against the wall, but why do you need things, little grappling hooks you pull around with you, tangled onto every other object, anyway, I wake up, which is the salient fact, and have no idea at first where i am or how long i've been here, it does come back, but slowly slowly, the acrid smell of my own sweat and skin, dark stains, and coagulated dribble down the side of my face gone cold and sticky against the concrete floor, and a trickling sound, a sheet of water slowly slowly coursing down the wall from the angle with the ceiling, i sit up, that's enough an inside voice speaks for me, that's enough for now

it takes a week, near enough, before the pieces fall back into place, though i am sure i have blank sheets in there somewhere, i am lucky i found this space before, or i'd have been gliding in the dark through the city, prey to who knows what, who knows who, wiped, so i guess i can count myself lucky i was just lying in this space, no more than a blocked corridor really, until whatever it was in my head my blood got washed out, and then the thirst, of course the thirst but i don't look any worse than most people after a long weekend out, so when i climb up onto the roof, and across in the sun, hand held sideways in front of my eyes, which don't seem to be able to shut down right now, i realize down there it's all in a dim twilight, and up here out here everything is cut out of cardboard with scissors, and set against the craft paper skies, so hand over face, I stare across the rooftops and go slowly slowly down the metal ladder where i usually come in, and reach the lower roof, into the elevator machinery and down, service doors, exit signs, i am asking myself all the way, is this worth it? and getting no answer except get a drink get a drink so when i finally slip out onto the street the busy street without even checking all i can think is get to r get to r he'll have water of course he will that's who i sell it to, so *cosi cosa* i'll have to buy some back and even maybe get to see flossy don't make me laugh, he's such a puritan in his own way mister purity well he has a point, but only slightly so i get to r's and he lets me in but not into the backroom, i just fall back onto his couch with him crouched squatting at eye level staring at me with that told you so look but he gets out his crystal suntory whisky tumbler and polishes it off, then fills it up from a decanter and hands it over to me almost to me but pulls it back at the last moment and i look at him and he says silly girl then he lets me have it and i have to say it was the good stuff, the best, all clear and limpid and cold and very mesolithic, the good stuff, probably the same stuff i'd brought to him, and that's the trick isn't it, to sell people back the stuff they already bought off you once, but fair play, i only had myself to blame, no complaints, and it went straight through into me and i could feel it filling out my bones and skin and eyes and hair, flowing through arteries, veins, the four corners of my heart, loop out to the lungs breathe and on again, everything rinsed and lit by spotlights and i could feel every breath and hear it like wind coming down a tunnel, r just standing there nodding slowslowly, now he knew i'd be back again, and no more fecal transplants for me, the occasionally excellent meals notwithstanding, what's the use of that? when your head empties out and you lie in a pool of your own dribbling for days without end, and i asked myself or told myself somewhere between a question and a realization as it dawned on me, hey don't i have a place to sleep now? and it turned out i did

i took a bus today, which i said i never would again, not after last time, but the body has its rhythms and preferences and idly i walked up the steps and sat down, near the back, invisible to all as i gazed out of the window not quite if i can't see you, then you can't see me, more accurately if i'm not looking at you, then i don't care whether you're looking at me, until, snap, i look up and lock eyes with you and that's where the trouble starts, but not today, as i was saying, off down the avenues and across the streets then down, then across to the east river slopes, and the pontoons, i looked out and the sun was setting mid canyon, over in jersey, a little lower along every block until it was unbright enough to be gazed at, if it's not gazing at me, then all the songs went through my head about the sun, lazy old, fat old, ketamine, here comes the sun song about the sunshine, and it all glowed up and over, the buildings' façades turning to burning glass, flowing down the avenues like syrup in a golden jar, in that light really invisible, truly not there to any eye

so it was back to the banks, which i should take the time to describe to you, because no-one knows and everyone talks about them as though they'd been out there in person themselves, which is certainly not true, even though there's more boats than you can shake a stick at sometimes, they're all amateurs and i'm not making any big claims for myself, except i keep my eyes and ears open, and i have at least seen or done these things myself, so the big bergs are way out, way out off the shelf, maybe thirty miles, just floating there, and pretty much unattended, that's dangerous as hell and no-one goes that far, unless just to see the sight, to say they've seen it, a whole, it looks like, city of white walls, square cut coming straight up out of the water, then the explosions, the crashing off, the calving as huge chunks come shearing off, in slow motion, causing waves and broken swells, it's just too vast to even think about, it's all real, no enhancement out here, and coming down at you the size of a city block, some of the fools surf on the tsunamis, and here's where the companies make their money, setting up shop on these mini-mountains and roping them off, got to get the guards up by helicopter and then pull alongside, blow shards off with small charges and scoop the fragments, big as a bus, net them, tie them off and speed away, you try speeding off with a hundred tons of ice tied to the back, but always the low sea fog, especially in the summer, and hacking it off, hacking into smaller and smaller pieces, a car a bed a fridge a table, and finally they let us scavenge whatever gets stuck on sandbanks, hidden shoals, very few of these ventures can be bothered to hire actual pilots, though the clear channels can be learned, i have no idea, i reckon you'd need a good few years on the gig to glean any patterns, and by then it would have all changed anyway, so, your best chance is luck, superstition, repetition, and traveling light, so you scavenge what you can carry and slip into a backpack, and back to shore and wait till night and run through the streets, leaving trails of meltwater, footprints, cut it up, wrap it up, all you can carry, into this bar, that bar, this friend, that friend, chop it in half, take it off and finally just enough left to cradle against yourself, and take that where? take that home or take it up to r because you owe him for that last time, and this time he lets you into the backroom and you can sit with flossy for a while just a short while flossy seems to understand the ice, needs the ice, people can't survive without clean water animals no different neither, so flossy understands, yes but r understands, too, and so, right, yes, i understand too, and that's why i never liked going to r's, but

there's a couple or three things i'd like to set straight, not that i really care or worry what people think about me, who's people, anyway? new friends in a new town is what i say, but still, there's things you just want to get rid of, get out of yourself, off your chest, like people say, as if you might have a second more womanly bosom bunched up inside, choking you off, and the first of those things is why i stopped doing the medical experiments as j called them, despite the regular meals, despite the good water and last but not least despite the regular cash, and in the end it wasn't even an ethical decision, or even for understandable reasons of health though lord alone knows they did not do what it said in the fine print, quite the reverse, irregular heartbeat, hyper, rundown, jumpy and my face all covered in blotches like some embarrassing teenager, no it was the sudden realization that all this careful hygiene, all the washing, all the boiled food, all the laundered sheets and pajamas, bathrobes and pillows were never for my benefit, for our benefit, but were just whims for the penthouse crowd, up in their clouds with our blood, our precious excrement, our juices carefully squeezed out of us and filtered into them, down their throats, up their holes, or if you want to go further, siphoned out of their sperm banks and pumped into our wombs, what else would you expect? it's a wet splice world

that's the first thing, the second is about my little edge or ledge, the sliver of dry sometime concrete i'd found between two buildings, outside one and underneath the other, not on any plan, but if you think about it, between the plans, there's nothing not planned, buildings don't just grow up like mushrooms, so it follows that someone made this plan, someone carved out or had carved out for them these little emptinesses, all over the city, under, across, and by the side, and then it followed like winter after summer that people would find them, that people such as i would find their way in, solo or variously, into occupation, and thus fulfil a plan that was neither their own nor took account of them, and yet were known, awaited and entered in the great ledger of the city, so, as was perhaps part of the plan too and a serious warning, i had to move on, not because of the spartan conditions, or the difficulty of ingress and egress, but because i was beginning to feel comfortable and had taken my eyes off the ball, to lie in and sleep when i have to ought to be up and out and roving, eyes peeled and alert, as if! but not locatable, not part of a pattern, it was a weakness, i admit

and the last thing was saddest of all, because it acknowledges my failure, as when one foot is raised, so the other must stand firm, when i only want to fly, but cannot, which is related in an inverted kind of way to the purity of the water and my fight to keep clean inside and out, a losing battle i might add because of the mountain range of forces and obstacles and habitudes stacked against me by time and tides and entropy, but like every team with a traitor at its heart, it came back to myself in the end, my lack of vigilance, and my subterranean needs bubbling up, fired by the sun or the micro sharpening out in the sea lanes, you see i thought i was keeping up my infrequent visits to unload my cargo of precious water, like some samaritan, battered and bruised from the voyages, and only then, perhaps, would i allow a few moments reverie at r's place, or some other such as good as or almost identical, but sadly i have to report that it was my addiction to r's place and its certainties which fed my entire enterprise of carefree misadventure, sad but true

so here i stand, too charged with sharpness from the sea again, and all of that, running back up the banks and through the streets to the endpoint of just that backpack filled with melting ice and ringing on r's door, which he opens like some pasha waiting for his concubine, that would be me, but having come to terms, i let the evening take its course and handed over the ice, which r caressed appreciatively, distracted because he knew what i wanted, and i knew what he wanted for my wanting, but i am not supposed to draw attention to that, so i have to wait for him to sigh or make the assumption, my last chance, which i could try to deny, but not tonight, and so, he's such a bastard, he glides over to the backroom door and unlocks it, that shimmer of green light leaking out and i just push past and go in, waiting until he follows in that stupid fake silk teenage girl's dressing robe, and it all starts to look and feel tawdry, but wait, as the doorseal clicks shut and the heat and fug of the bathroom take over, i see the bath, the high glass wall like a fishtank, the tiles, and the movement within, and just get it over with and pull off my clothes, r is leaning against the door like he's waiting for a bus, or watching a band play, which i suppose he is, in a way, entertainment, and as i climb the steps and step into the tank, i can see him rubbing himself off under his robe, discreetly, does he think he's invisible? then flossy comes round the corner and suddenly i stop worrying, i stop caring about anything, there's just this here-and-now and she recognizes me, they say they can't but i know this one can, remembers me, and i slide to the bottom of the tank just my face and nostrils above the water, and flossy crawl-swims over and climbs up my body so delicately, her skin flashing in the green light, ripples of patterns like a swiftly written parchment, the words gone too fast to register, but it's all fine, her body firm but soft to the touch so gentle, the water clean and warm, i take a deep breath and sink to the bottom, entwined and remember again what it is like to drift buoyed in the sea, remember to forget this children's nonsense tale of walking and breathing on dried earth, solid ground, as a tentacle traces the line of my cheekbone and lifts a slow wisp of hair from my face and i stroke her delicate head soft as a soothing breast on my breast and hold onto my only oldest dearest friend and familiar and no-one can see me crying

it must have been full moon, because dreams, because heat, because sweating, because fear, but nothing now, no dense undergrowth of dread between each breath, the ear cocked and held in silence, waiting for the twig to crack outside the window, or some unseasonable mechanical noise, off in the distance, just calm, slow down heartbeat, calm, it's just the wind, calm, then saying calm, finally saying I

Coda:

i had a dream, i was back out in the ice fields, only it was at night, deep and moonless, the strangest thing, no sounds at all, not even the motor on the back of the zodiac, we were just gliding along between the bergs, black waters and a glow on the horizon from the ice field, from the floodlights perched on top, and the waterfalls of mist pouring off, sublimated, up above a sky deeper than velvet dotted with sprayed milk, wheeling overhead as we drifted around corners, icewalls rearing up ahead, alongside, behind, reflections of all the stars in the deep water, and the cold cold breeze chilling your face, bare arms, the wake under the boat silver, i trail a hand in the water and it feels warm, i know it isn't but i feel it warm, like blood, like running my hand over the body, stroking, being through the water, when we grind to a halt at the foot of a giant cliff, going up into the sky dripping dripping, but i can't hear it, like a music just beginning beneath hearing, seeing the rhythm as the drops hit the still water and ripple the stars, i cup my hands and bring the water to my mouth and look down, in the depths a streak of white movement, fish, something side to side, and in the dream i step over the side of the boat and let myself slip into the water, sink down, not needing to breathe now, turning turning and looking up at the underskirts of the iceberg, all intricately sculpted, circle upon circle upon ellipse, interlocking carvings as far as you can look, like little roofs, as if scooped out by hand by generations of musalman artisans, how did that happen? and i feel a touch along my shoulder, turn, it's alright, turn and awaken.

the one about hibernation

FROM THE WINDOW, you could not tell. Just another snow day in Manhattan. Staring down at the street, flakes falling slowly and the blanket of silence. Nothing moving. But little by little, as it dawns, the absence of cars, the presence of birds, sparrow, pigeon and starling, black scrawl of tree branch, other birds. Who knows? some rodent scuttling, but not at this hour, too vulnerable now to hawk, the black rat.

Time enough to stare at the ceiling, in the grey grey, some real or imagined steam howling through the heating system. Reach out the arm, scalding to the touch, there's change. Meaning she chose well, in that time, when time? then time. The watch is expensive and battered, stopped. The time reads 3.58, two minutes to four, night or day? stopped. Ha, she says, under her breath, 'right twice a day'. Hearing the low breathing next to her, she stiffens, now fully awake. Stops her own breath and listens. Nothing. Only imagining, or? then one slow exhale, the warmth behind, knees behind her own knees behind a bulge under the bedclothes, slowly rising and falling, too slow, he's gone, away, he, huge.

But the better not to take a chance, she rolled slowly slowly like a trapped mouse playing dead, pushed a leg out from under the covers, up on one elbow, paused, then slowly sitting upright, peering into the room.

Strange room, gathering darkness, it's dusk not dawn what difference? out of the bed, the room, the bedroom and draw the door to behind her but no tell-tale click of the lock to dive through the fog, self-preservation alerting even the deepest diver that a predator, or what, might be in the room, no not even that. In the passage, cold tiles. The toilet seat glacial and the pee will not come. How long? A day. Two days? a week, in here, up here, the cold streets, the warm apartment. Whatever he is, whoever he was, will be, right now, dressing in his living room, lights out, no light, the long corridor outside in blackness. Still water in the pipes. To drink to drink. Maybe three days, then. Sit staring at the wall. Stupor. What are all these? Books. Keep the cold out, warmth in. Insulation. Piled against the windows, merest foxhole to spy out, and down through the flurries, white on white.

In the bedroom, he turns over. Bed creaks. Pirate ship becalmed, hemp rigging creak. Pull on your boots girl and get out of there. Should the giant awaken, there will be hell to pay, his hell, or yours. The knife could end that, but then what, where to dispose of the body? and why? one of the splendid ironies, the steam heating is still running in the socially disadvantaged warren, while on the ritzy glitzy side of town, it's all empty, frigid, a shuttered beehive.

Boots on. Coat. There's an Indian blanket over the armchair by the curtains, perhaps a distant descendant from the typhus ridden gifts presented to the Sioux to help them on their way west. Tie it on. Mask. Hat. Out.

In the corridor, pull the door as closed as it can go. Regrets, but the price to pay.

Her hands, her fingers, striped each one in black, as tattoos, or girlhood rings, hooped, some faded, others crisp, dozens.

A box of matches found by touch, struck and along the corridor a shuffled step at a time until the match sizzles out. Three strikes to the stairwell, the heavy door clanging, echoing behind her. Now down the flights, three steps at a time, running, falling, and through the last barrier onto the street.

Heavy mittens now, and a hunch into the doorway. Ô the silence. Ô the snow. A foot and a half deep. And there, in the middle of the street, just the single track of a vehicle's tires. Just the one.

Her eyes flicker, to the left and the right, nothing but snow and quiet, the car tracks still defined with treadmarks, she sets off, following the trail as it bears right and northward, up University, dissolving into whiteness three blocks ahead.

The car tracks headed in a snake around the blocks, doubling back eastward to the village. Broadway passed in a blizzard, the wind ripping south across from Strand, whose doorway bore the discreet pink ribbon.

J crossed the road, halting in the middle to bow to the cardinal points. Nothing, nothing, nothing, and nothing. Then dragging the front door of the bookstore open, slipped inside.

The sound of the wind dropped suddenly, muffled by the carpet and the short entryway. J stood in the lobby, a trail of powdered snow not reaching even the first table stacked with bestsellers. The light fell off, leaving the back of the room in darkness. Small gusts rattled the door and shook the windows. J shivered and walked deeper into the store, sniffing the air for its comfort of old books, print, ink, must, her footsteps deadened.

Stood slumped over, shoulders aching, harder to breathe, after just a few hundred yards of walking. Sit down. On the staircase by the elevators. Sit down, doubled over, hands on knees, head between hands, wrapped up against the cold, in the dark.
when
the shop is crowded, full of people, deafening footfall, chatter and laughter. It is, what? coming up to Christmas. She's doubled up, blocking the stairs. 'You OK?' he asks, and J looks up to see a quizzical young man wearing a knitted Peruvian hat. Alpaca or Guanaco, the kind with ear-flaps. 'I like your hat', J says, 'I should get one like that'.

Three students pushing past cause J to stand and move to one side. Alpaca boy smiles and squeezes next to her. 'They itch like fuck, unfortunately', he says, 'feels like you got fleas'.

'Do they have fleas in the Andes?' He laughs, 'Not any more. They exported them all in these fucking hats'. They laugh. Hundreds of people. Hot, hot. Wrapped up, badly, against the cold. J can see that now. Expensive and fashionable jackets, not even warm enough for skiing; tight cotton pants that cling to the girls' legs. Some boots, some designer housewear. Good enough for the short dashes between house and subway, subway and store, and restaurant, then home. All be dead after a night outdoors. J takes off her gloves and examines her hands, the black rings drawn around her fingers. The young man nods towards them, 'What's that? Tribal?'
J 'Sort of', a way of passing the time.

J rubs her hands together, turns them over. I know you like I know the back of my own hand. Do you? Know the back of your own hand? Or the palm, for that matter?

J imagines that, an identikit parade of knuckles, phalanges, and nails bitten to the quick, or manicured, like okra, or spatulate, reddened by the cold, or hypoxic under the nails, blue. Bitter almonds. These mine? His? Hers? Theirs? The folds, the glow, the blains. No? Not sure? Not me? My? then the urchin mitts, hieroglyphed, zebras, dirt under the nails, grubby, lightly scabbed. Mine.

Clap.

Dark. No-one there now. Puddle of melted snow under her feet. Cold, but not that cold. My hands are cold. I can say this without fear of contradiction, though no further inferences may be made. This is today's one corner of the Universe to stand on, and with a strong enough lever, to move the heavens. In an emptied bookshop.

Clap.

So what can she learn, and learn anew each day, each segment of days, as the winter gets deeper, the astonishing become rote; the rote, ingrained. And then change, nothing is holding its center, the centrifuge still spins, even as we wander around our islands, just waiting for the roundabout to stop.
But not quite now. We say, 'Not now. I'm not ready yet'. And that's true, not ready. But the yet has to be dealt with sooner rather than later. O.K. Not tonight though. I'm alone here, I don't need to justify this, make up some story, some song & dance to keep you entertained, away from the edge of the building, from the edge of the rooftop. But the snow is so soft. Yes, I said, but it's a permanent solution to a temporary problem, and she

said back, your problem is you are all patched together with temporary solutions to permanent problems. Still, I didn't jump; she did. So who's laughing now? I was laughing all the way down, she says, couldn't you hear me. Finally. And you? You're crying all the time. That's why you love the rain, because nobody can see you, and this snow, because there is nobody left to see you. Crying.

The store is dark the store is cold and there's nothing to eat in here, the drink machines long emptied, the pipes frozen, bathrooms in disarray. No providential steam radiators in here. And no people. Funny. There's enough rooms in the city now for everyone. Look out at the street, mist the glass of the front door. Long twilight. And those car tracks, blurred over now, maybe they were headed in the opposite direction anyway. Now the compass is set to the East, a few blocks at a time, you can sneak into most buildings, or if you feel adventurous and don't mind the risks, break into a new one.

I mean an old one. All sealed up. It could be empty. Or it could be full of something that needs to be kept locked in. A tricky call. Hence the knife, hence the caution. Hence making sure you are awake before you do that. Ultimately, hence the pink ribbons. Signifying that the door is open and the building 'safe'. (We all hold our sides in a grotesque mime of happy laughter. Looks more like a fit. Bresson said, or something like this: never show people having paroxysms, in which everybody is exactly alike.) meaning, someone has been here before and might still be inside, take it or leave it. City etiquette demands we not eat each other, and the democracy of the freeze has wiped out not only any morality of intimacy, but frankly, any play of personal like, desire, or volition. Crossing the doorway is a big, fat, unequivocal Yes to the world, with its equivocal, petty, simplistic imperatives.

We all want warm, want water, want to sleep when we need to, without having the throat slit, without asking permission, without needing to talk, the death of language, then as a bad job, and even movement, what do I know, just don't defecate in the bed; and the body has its wants, now so thankfully freed of the head, can obtain them so easily, and then sleep and then awaken, and then out into the streets again, shrug and walk off, everything owned, is tied to the body, or in coat pockets, some times a small sack, but ostentatious, that, and liable to draw attention.

Clap.

J walks east on 12th street, along the middle of the road. Perhaps, must be, eyes watching, idly, no-one will shout or be heard. Today, she may make her ten blocks before exhaustion. These streets she knows. Knew.

Here, at the junction of Second and 13th, the snow has been melted, some heat pipes run too close to the surface here, how can they still function? dimly the old scientific questions pose themselves again. Parts of the city run on automatic, until and unless they break down, could last weeks months years... years, maybe not, but the cold season. And here's the rub, it's been too long. Even counting for a long winter and a delayed spring, we should be out of it by now... or are the calculations all wrong? I know how many sleeps, but not how many nights... groups of days, then dead time. Even the minimum. When did I last see the moon? And no-one to tally with. And why would I? To throw the ball into the future and say to myself, 'Why, only a few weeks left. Just a few more days.' A single crescent moon, hanging drunken off the plough. But that's not true.

I should say something about my tally system. It's very ancient, being based on the Old Brythonic 'score' which may or may not have been an actual method for counting herds of sheep used by er shepherds, but it's a nice way of counting big abstract numbers that have to be apprehended quickly. You can try it on starlings in the sky. Or you can adapt it, as I have, to measure time when you have no idea no continuity of its passing. I don't know if I am the only one who developed such a method. Probably not. But, having said that, I never told anyone I met. I want to keep that edge working in my favor. It's just that by now, so much time must have passed, it's clear to me that spring is not going to return us to normal. I know this winter has already lasted at least four months. And that's a minimum. The dull problem at the heart of it all is no-one knows how long they sleep for. It could be a normal night, or a long night. But it could equally be two days, sleep away your Sundays, as many of us used to after the Fraturday partying. Or a week, when you wake up, barely, with a completely dry mouth, aching throat, urge to urinate but somehow thinner legs, unsteady gait, and still the curtains are drawn, the skies dim. It could have been a month. I don't know how long you can sleep without drinking, but I know what it feels like to spend the first ten minutes drinking like an old-time horse at its trough. So, what to do? First, get a good timepiece, a mechanical one that you need to wind up. Some of those can keep going for about two days. Which isn't perfect, because if you wake up and it's stopped, OK, you know you have been out for at least two days. But, still, it could be twenty... and versy-vicey, if you wake up and it's still ticking – if you are, too – then it means it isn't two days yet... but by winding it back up, you can make a pretty good guess, you get a feel for it. Of course, some of the old watches have day and date windows, which is just too much to ask, isn't it? All you have to do is note the date when the watch stops and reset to 1 again. Anyway, it's imprecise, but actually not too bad. If you estimate a week, odds are it's probably somewhere between five and ten days. And it cancels out, under- and over- estimates.

So, then, I take out my trusty marker pen and draw a black ring around the base of my little finger, where it joins the hand. That's one week. Leaving a small gap, I start counting the next week, and when I'm satisfied, another ring on the same finger. You can get eight rings on a single finger, that's two full months.

Oh, moons. Yes, you rarely get to see a moon, because of the clouds and whatnot, but when I do see a moon, I'll draw a little cartoon of it next to the nearest ring, so I can correct by factoring in the phases of the moon. I'm pretty sure I know the difference between sleeping for three days or five weeks, so that's another corrective. And working like that, there's room for about a year on one hand. You can almanac a full year (which might be only eight months, or as long as sixteen months, of course) on one hand. And you have two hands.

Unless you used to have one of those old Rolexes and someone cut your hand off to steal it. In which case only one hand. Do you now immediately feel sorry for all of those one-handed guys? Don't. It's obscene to have one of those watches and keep it to yourself, hidden under your gloves, hands tucked into the pockets hoping that no-one will see it, except for those other ones who've got one too... ah but can you imagine the exquisite toils of meanness in working out who makes the first move? Getting comfortable enough to even think of falling asleep?

People are so stupid. Because the truth is, there are so many more one-handed people who find themselves in that situation not because one of the street scum snuck in, overpowered them, and then performed (think about this, now) some kind of impromptu surgery to steal the timepiece. A myth. Why not just slip the band off the wrist? or if force and threats are to be used, just get the wretch to hand it over. Or whack them with a brick. You don't need a surgical machete to obtain a watch. No. Most of the one-handed are so because they were caught trying to steal a watch, and had their hand taken as punishment. Right? Wrong. If someone is caught stealing a watch, inside a building, a building full of people who actually live there, they are not going to fuss about administering any kind of nuanced punishment, no, just the one kind, and kill them there and then. No-one has time for amputations. Still, you do see a lot.

But to get back to my system, why am I so sure that this winter has dragged on too long? Because my right-hand fingers are covered in black rings and moon phases, and my left (writing) hand is covered in faded bands, a palimpsest showing at least three years. Give or take a year. And my hair is down my back, and everyone I ever meet, though they are mostly asleep, resembles also some mediaeval Japanese warlord. And the men's beards.

Hence you will appreciate, here, that I am out walking. I drank a gallon of water in the apartment. I am starving. The guy up there is deep deep asleep and there's no way I am going back up there again. Lucky knows when it's lucky.

There are some watches I've heard about that have moon phases on them, but I've never seen one, so I'm going to say that's just one of those stories people tell to shut you up and get you into bed with them, because if somebody knows something like that, and they've got a warm bed and a locked door to prove it, what are you waiting for? how bad could it be? and you can always cut their throat and steal their watch if they get uppity.

It's an error to assume your brain is what keeps your body under control, or the mind, if you prefer. Take walking in the snow, for example, it's too taxing, too vexing, and too numbing for a mind to stay focused on the simple lowering and raising of the feet. The balance in this slow falling forward doesn't need to go up so high, it shouldn't be weighing on the thought processes at all, and in reality, like the diplodocus, it doesn't, each step sends a shudder though the leg muscles up to the hip, and you list sideways, do it again, right left, left right, the perfect feedback loops go down to the other foot, the next, leaving the torso and arms to automatically counter-swing, keeping the center of gravity in a lazy arc, damped harmonic motion, only requiring a fresh impulse, maintain the rhythm, and no input from the head, which is free to wander its own realms, take in the surroundings, capture the lack of distinct odors, it's another day, and I feel as though I am on some high hypoxic mountain, I once read about mountaineers using all their concentration to put one foot in front of the other, to keep breathing in out in out, all uphill of course, although a curious fact is that the vast majority of deaths (on Mount Everest, for example) occur on the descent, probably from cumulative exhaustion as, by definition, coming back down requires you to have gone up beforehand, not to mention that falling down going uphill is a shorter ask than 'watch that first step it's a doozy' going down, which is also where the avalanches are, not that I'd give anyone advice get to the top...then stay there, any more than it's a useless statistic to know that most injuries occur at home, so get out of the house isn't necessarily the way to avoid most injuries, I digress, I am saying, like a mountain climber, the brain is not what's required on a methodical foot slog, the nerve ganglia at the base of the spine will do that just as well, though as ever we are talking metaphors here and neither humans nor terrible lizards have brains, even auxiliary brains, in their ass. Dinosaurs, in harmony with horses, don't even have asses.

I walk along the streets, the snow comes and goes in my mind, it's impossible to hold an idea out there because this is not Happy Christmas snow for building models or even toy igloos, or having snowball fights with your friends, it's the beginning of tundra climate, and you cannot spend more than a few minutes outdoors without risking perishing, a correct use of the world for once, but 'to go through' what exactly?

In passing as those uncontrolled thoughts bang around inside my head, just like left right left right, as would have been ironic only a few moons ago, that is – in this time of undeniable global warming why has everything become so cold, and secondly, was erecting all those temporary or virtual icebergs a form of involuntary sympathetic magic to call down all of this ice upon ourselves? or as a former girlfriend once said, am I a bad patch in your relationship? or are you a bad patch in mine? referring, unspokenly, to the third corner of our little triangle. They were a bad patch in mine, as it did turn out, which is another way of saying keep your eye on the ball, there's three sides to every triangle.

As I walk down this street, I am assailed by memories, yet they are not my memories, I was not, could not have been here, rather they are the memories engendered by the street, filtered through you, or me, or another, hovering waiting to be picked up by the next vessel to pass, tuned into the right frequency, the lump of coal, the rheostat, the crystal set, as this, tramping down mid street, I glide past a window, gone dark, and see the painting displayed, the one that showed me even our bodies are not of a piece, they are just a loose alliance of muscle and bones, held barely together with tendon and sinew, each moving independently, with its own agenda and trajectory, a miracle of balance and fluid dynamics, how can we dare to walk? when it's all about alignments of force, we could so easily collapse, a quivering pile of femur and ulna, never to rise again, yet we run, we dance, we flee, I can't remember the image, yet the red, the black, the brown earth and sky, I recall the painting in the window so crystal sharp with its redbrown body tracings arcs with the whitebones of history, mounted on those other bodies, distended now and lolloping over the imagined plains to the Mississippi heedless of Indians or buffalo, dust tamped down. A naked rider on a human skeletal horse, suggesting the plains of Oklahoma here on the Lower East Side (Loisaida), one hand on the invisible bridle, the skull with blinkers, blinders, literally scratched out the eyes, that basic stirrup, invention which supercharged the Mongols all across the horizontal continent of Eurasia, while in the vertical Americas, people had to continually dismount to plot and plant new agriculture, twisted isthmus, making every lesson that much harder to be learnt, passively.

Or if the image is not me or you but all of us, I remember (how can I remember?) the Chilean madman Alejandro Jodorowsky, re-invented as a comic book magus, dispensing his wisdom in heartwarming slices of video, turning over cards of the Marseille tarot, to the rapt, ever rapt attentions of the Platonic Audience. I see a man in a white summer suit being fed fresh strawberries by a young woman half his age or less, Don Alejandro, keeping one step ahead of the bailiffs and the politically correct style police. But he has many ideas, not only walking in a straight line through Valparaiso, one of which is to view the Family as a single amoeboid organism which sprawls over several generations, back to that painting, as the rider must surely fall from such a not-quite-connected assemblage of bone, muscle, and mesentery. Solid, liquid, and where's the soul at? Is it a fractal, immune to resolving?

That in such families, which coalesce and break apart and recombine dynamically, droplets racing down a windscreen, over five or six generations, the traumas and cowardice of early individuals might manifest in the youngest, often the weakest, or a central obsession suddenly break out in an outlier, like a jetblack child appearing to the astonishment of a venerable landed white family in the deep south. Something like karma, but apparently unconnected to the recipient. The Victorian great-grandmothers violation leading to the stubborn misanthropy of the steampunk teenager; the thwarted, muscle-bound fathers producing hyper-neurotic sons who faint in summer. Or after a hundred years or more of mediocrity, suddenly out of nowhere, a golden child, all sunshine and light. Well, that wasn't exactly me. Looking at the painting I could see the fall into the dust was already inscribed by the haunches that had attempted to spring, but slipped their purchase, and were already tumbling before today's mistakes had even been aligned. That's a lot to charge a half-glimpsed painting with. It must have been a good one. Or maybe an album sleeve, I don't know. This street, then.

I had a friend who once worked down here, he was a simple guy, didn't think things out too deeply, but his heart was in the right place, fell foul of the cruel orthomorphía craze that came and went a few years back, when people still had jobs or still looked for them, and in the end, once everyone else had been filtered out, how to choose among the thousand of folks left standing for each petty post? why, by how they look, of course, and this boy, so fine, so compact, no facial hair, a neutral but very pleasant face, let it be said no-one ever knew if he presented as Chinese, or Vietnamese, or Indonesian or Filipinx, Andean, or Native American... he used to keep a mental note of who he'd been mistaken for each week, but as I say, very pleasant, and very pleasant looking, and learned the requirements for this one job (which involved something unattainably difficult like standing all day behind a reception desk all day, blending in with marble and silence all day each day) to wit: more symmetry, which to be honest he already had, to an extreme, which led him to the conclusion that what they really wanted was a girl, but not precisely that, what they promised him was that if he could 'even himself up' a little, nothing could stop him from moving to the top of the waiting list, he didn't need a nose job, or facial work of any kind, and his deep black eyes (he worked on that gaze with his digitalis eyedrops) gave him a kind of perfection, no, not the face, it was circumcision, and how they knew he wasn't circumcised, well, they had to look, I suppose, anyway, they told him to snip away, thousands do, otherwise an unsightly and uneven bulge would appear, would never hang down straight and even, and at first he thought they meant cut off the whole thing, to which, No, but they merely wanted even his invisible cock to dress small and symmetrical, neither to the right nor to the left, and to my everlasting shame, he acquiesced and did as he was told, that's the wrong word acquiesce, it's their word, he used 'agreed', at his own charge, and it wasn't 'told' or even 'suggested', it was a more amorphous feeling of 'they would have preferred not to be made uncomfortable by having felt obliged to manifest their disquiet in a subtle yet palpable feeling of awkwardness', which is quite a mouthful for a vague ambiance, and I say 'caved in', to his everlasting upset, and they never gave him the job anyway, though he may indeed have reached top of some notional interim list or ranking for a brief moment, but that's another story and also another street that neither of us walks along any more.

I had walked there before, others had walked there before, the street itself was, is, and will be there, the place it is, and all of this can be read, or felt, that's what draws us to cities, and why the beauty of the mountains or the sea feels so inhuman, though no less affecting for all that. Is it any wonder you cannot hold fast to place, untouched by the pull of tides?

But that's not how it is, or how it was, just how I fear it will be.

With all that calculation, none of it helps. It's snowing, or it's not snowing, the roads might be clear, or drifts might engulf you at every corner. What's certain is that the angles are all softened by the snow, the noises all subdued under a foam, and however many steps you think you can manage, you find yourself automatically counting inside your head, until only the numbers are real, seventy-five, seventy-six, and you have to get back inside, in a doorway, in an alley, out of the wind, out of the cold, snowblind and blinking.

The street door has a twist of faded orange plastic tied off around the handle, left over right over left, under through pull, twist, tighten. A shape we all recognize to designate a semi-occupied building, possibly not fatal—the yellow 'out' tag has been removed—meanwhile the snow has stopped falling but not the wind, which is blowing powder across the roads, piling up on the south sides, howling down the avenues, then these little peaceful eddies around trees, some bare railings, a kerb stone visible, as if this were only one bad winter night, and as long as you don't turn around to see the entire side of a tower block hung with icicles, you might believe that. Whatever else you might believe, and the increasing monomania tells you it's freezing your brain again, and all you can think about is the stepping, counting obsessively from one to two and back to one again, until you cross the road and reach the door. Metal door, might only be an electric junction box inside, or steps down to the trash basement (you take that, temporarily), but there's a feeling to this that there's more. The door is set back a foot from the sidewalk, and drifted shut, a good sign, no-one has come in or out for days, which could mean the building is empty, or that everyone's truly in slumber. Digging out quickly and quietly isn't so important these days, there's really no-one around to surprise you, but you don't get over the reflex, that's why it's a reflex, and scratch at the ice, chip into the corners, kick with the toes of your boots and tug, tug until the steel door crunches open, just enough to let you in sideways and the last gesture before pulling it well closed, is to rip off the orange tag so no-one knows it's free and slam the door well shut behind you.

Of course, a neophyte might have forgotten to lift the tag in their haste, but you won't be troubled too much by neophytes. I remember once being told that word meant a new plant, and then it meant someone in a religious convent. And now it means someone who doesn't know enough to survive one winter. Ah. Words drift like snow.

The slam deadens everything, the wind drops to a distant howl, the light falls to zero, the faintest glow across the room, under the crack of an interior door, a staircase and out into a lobby.

It's clean in here, and quiet. There's even carpeting across to the front doors, buried and glowing pale gray with the light through head-deep drifts. No footsteps, not even dirty ones, unless someone has taken the time and effort to mop&glow the floor over there. The carpets spotless. I try the light switches, but no dice.

After the half days spent tramping the streets, the lobby's muffled whine sounded as though one had gone deaf. If you didn't move, there was nothing at all, anechoic, or the blood in your ears and a hyperawareness of the sounds of almost silent breathing. More, it was as though a particularly minimalist sound artiste had laid individual sounds just so over a totally void backdrop, omitting the roomtone. Some movements passed by as if in outer space, while others fractured into intact elements, the rub of a boot on carpet, the click of the same shoe on marble, a brief squeal as rubber met rubber, then nothing, nothing, nothing but a single metallic click as you close a door gingerly.

Clap.

She stepped over to the wall of mailboxes and stopped before them. Mittens laboriously pulled off with the teeth, webbed fabric whistling. Un-scratch a pocket flap and pull out a small bunch of keys, chained to a thick leather thong. Ruffle through the keys and grasp the tiniest between thumb-tip and forefinger-tip, fit it into the lock of the mailbox and turn: a discrete scrape, then:

'Keys? Haven't had much call for keys for quite a while.' The voice guttural, forceful, but out of practice, undermining its strength with a croak and a falter. The speaker cleared his throat, 'I mean, people don't really drop in uninvited any more'.

J turned round and saw the man, silhouetted against the front wall-window, a tall and bulky shape like some bear. Also, between J and the entry door, and well-placed to stop a dash to the stairs. Stairs up, anyway, a bad tactical move. How many neophytes froze to death on rooftops? Stand and fight was the sad but true lesson. But perhaps it would not come to that.

J drew the key out of the lock and turned slowly to face the stranger. He was twice her size. But hadn't moved an inch. How to interpret? Was he ungainly and recently out of torpor? Could be. But he lacked the tell-tale sway of the freshly awoken. But he could be clumsy, too. On the other hand, some of those big guys could be surprisingly nimble and it could have been luck that he was in the optimal position to block her any attempt to escape, though that could have been luck. He was after all just standing in the middle of a lobby. But she hadn't heard him arrive and that was either a rare lapse, or evinced skill on his part. So let's dance, J thought, and moved very calmy but decisively toward the staircase, trying to trace a slow semi-circle around the obstructing figure. He was breathing, his breath condensed on the air, somewhat labored, too, why had J not registered that sound till then. His eyes followed J as she shifted to the right, but his head did not turn, nor his torso move.

The next step will do it, thought J knowing she would then find herself closer to the door she had entered by, than the man, shifting her weight to her right leg so she could—and that's when the man sprang, one swift leap to his left, grabbing J with both padded arms and carrying them both to the floor, where his weight immobilized her. He very rapidly folded his right knee in to pin J's hips to the floor, while his upper body weight lay on his forearm, pressed across her collar bone and pressing down on J's throat. She twisted and struggled, but very quickly decided to play dead. The man didn't move, but his face was right up against hers, deep set brown eyes, and an animal mass of facial hair. Plenty of time to think now. And to decipher the smell off him. 'sh, sh, sh... I'm not going to hurt you. Just...' J twisted, the man held her down, 'Sh!'.

J shushed. Face to face.

The man changed position, again, very suddenly, there goes the hope that he was barely awake, more like he'd been alert and waiting, J was mentally retracing her route into the room, where he could have, must have been for her not to have noticed him. Probably in the stairwell.

So: behind her as she came in. He had heard her efficient break-in and entry, and had just mirrored her own move, in a semi-circle behind her back. He could have instantly overpowered her, but he'd waited to see what she would do, and what she'd done is play her hand, reveal that she possessed a mailbox key. With only the very slightest of chances that he'd not understood what that fact implied. But he had. The man, J's throat clamped in his left hand, began an efficient rifling through her parka pockets until his fingers closed on the lanyard and yanked out the keychain. But even with the sharpest of pulls, the leather did not snap.

"It won't..." the man's hand clamped down on her mouth. Why?

He shook his head rapidly, then slowly released his muzzling.

"It's got a steel cable inside. You can't snap it." More information than he needed. Now he needed some cutters. The idea of a defensive strategy is generally to keep people away from weapons, if you can. By this mis-step, J had lost perhaps thirty seconds in the struggle and chess play, and it struck her of a sudden why he had let her go, why he wanted her to keep quiet. And why he was not dressed for the streets. There must be others. And the man did not want the others to find J. At least, visibly, he didn't want them to find her yet. Which seemed a good idea to J, too, as it meant there was only one body to dispose of. She'd done it before, and she could do it now.

Clap.

It's not so easy, and the man was behaving oddly. As alert as you like, watchful, yet somehow not quite there. Staring off into some other world, dragged back if I tried to move. Stronger than me, certainly, but maybe I could catch him off balance. I'm wiry. Dragging me over to the mailboxes, opening my box, the correct one first try, and ramming his fingers inside, scooping out my treasures. Such treasures. I can see his look of incomprehension at the objects in his hand. He wasn't getting it at all. Maybe he thought I had some food in there, or sugar, or batteries. At any rate, he was disappointed and angry enough to thrust his hand into my face.

What's this? 'Keys,' I said. What else could I say? A boxful of keys that held a dozen potentially safe houses. Not that he cared. But maybe the one in this building? My place? Hardly. But a room that I knew was locked and empty. The weak link in the whole tactical chain, of course, was getting the bunch out of the mailbox in this lobby. Too valuable to carry around, too risky to hide, thought I'd found the perfect compromise. I had. But I had not kept up my vigilance, and so... now being pushed and dragged up the emergency stairs to the fourth floor, to see what I had hidden, what could usefully be bargained, or used as a distraction. Still warming up, and working out where this guy's weak points were, apart from the fact that he hadn't killed me, or even tried to, really.

I didn't ask myself the question, 'Can he read?' but it became evident that he could read numbers when he dragged me up three flights of stairs to reach the corridor which leads to the door whichfor which I had a set of keys, third floor, 333, three keys, top bolt, bottom bolt, and heavy tumbler in the middle. I like to think of it as badger-like security, shut the place up tight, no ingress or egress, no keys: no entry, and the keys in a box guarded by other keys, in other buildings. Just unlucky this time, enough time to refine my methods, if I survive, never hide the keys in the same building, and never write the numbers on the fobs. But then again, in the tradition of, and on the principles of angry street robbers, the so-called muggers, I was told, in the first days, when to be attacked or held up was still considered an unfortunate stroke of misfortune, always carry a little spare change, in case the perpetrator, pumped up on adrenaline or whatever artificial courage and despair necessary to cross that line, would vent his or her anger, let's be fair, on the badly chosen victim, who was such a loser that not only did they venture out into parts of town they shouldn't oughtta, but they'd also been stupid enough to have nothing worth stealing, either. You get stabbed just for being so lame. You'd lose your coat and shirt that way. Far better to have a mock wallet or money clip with a few tens in it. A shrug. A cut. Come out with more, the next time! Hell, in São Paulo, they steal people's swimwear and flip-flops. And for god's sake don't wear a ring that's too tight on your finger. More natural history here: if a guy has hands studded with rings, don't mess with him, you can be sure someone, somewhen has tried to persuade them off him, and if he has ten fingers, for sure someone else doesn't. This guy was wearing mittens, so you never can tell. I had to open my own door, though, and I would say it pushed back with a satisfying oomph, but the fact that it had clearly remained undisturbed felt like a betrayal. If someone had gotten inside, maybe through the broken window, and soiled and fouled everything, I would have felt a grim ironic 'told you so', but no—here was my own home, safe and sound and now invaded by some hulk of a moron that I hadn't worked out could or could not read. He slammed the door shut and spun the deadbolt. That's seriously quality hardware. New York's finest handcrafted tumbler mechanism. But the room was different. And what do I mean when I say Mine? It wasn't mine. I don't know what anyone means when they say 'Mine'. Unless it's mine eyes, which, having been around since your birth, can at least claim legitimate association. Which isn't the same thing, of course. But an apartment? It certainly hadn't been part of my life since time immemorial. Five years, more like, on & off. Rented, then persisted, then squatted, then abandoned, then reclaimed, then preserved like a deep secret. I call it Mine. And now it's not mine, or not mine alone. Not His yet, and heaven forfend, never Ours, though that's what he was probably thinking. Ours. I get the key, the room, and the girl. Except...

Who wrote those stories? And why did anyone believe them. The boys did, in so far as they had gaping holes in their psyches. The girls? Holes, holes. Holes everywhere. The relationship between farmer and pig. Why descend to the level of the farmer? And who, what, why, stoop to choose the level of the pig? Who pig? There is a lot of work that just never gets done. And now here we are, two people alone together in a room in a building that neither of us can link with any pronouns, possessive or otherwise, not belonging.

It seems like a whole age since we entered the corridor. Yes, I can open the front door, No, the apartment is not occupied, I saw the leaf I placed in the door jamb flutter down harmlessly, but also, no, the room is not intact.

Over in the corner by the bed, a window is out, the curtain pulled back. What? some intruder, once? the snow creeps in, blown in a drift against the sill and falling into the room, puddled, refrozen. There's no heating up here, the bedclothes stiff with frost, no more haven, but here we are. Set standing in a half light, at the moguls of frozen and re-frozen snow dust, or for the late lamented Eskimo extended vocabulary, as erroneous as the name itself. But we'll need more names for snow now, and evermore.

A lot of grunting and pointing, what have I to say? to set against that? I should be so lucky to have no bones broken, or curse my own stupidity in failing to evade the obvious feints. Doesn't it always boil down to this? I didn't expect to be surprised. So tense and alert when nothing is happening, dim and dozy when the door opens and the fiendish stranger just walks in. The order of events a little different, I know, for everyone. But this is basic genetic folly. We can't stay alert all the time. The gaps in our waking are the gaps others spot and exploit. I have a hard time holding onto a solid drawn line of consciousness, cause and effect mixed up. He didn't surprise me, I allowed surprise to intrude; I wasn't vigilant, no-one was laboring to pierce my vigil. One of those moments when every analysis breaks down itself, the antibodies attacking their own host. And then sleep, you can't exclude sleep. We say it's an effect of the weather, but as likely it's the cause. It's cold outside, but not arctic; it's dim, but not dark; there's snow, but it's not a glacier. I wonder if maybe I could just walk out, carefree, kicking up the ice needles, as a sun peeps through the overcast. Some birds, some distant rumble, normalcy. Like that military Uncle slapping you on the back and throwing you into a stream, laughing, it'll make a man of you, or a woman, whichever is the current preferred slogan. Are

You Army Strong? I know I am not. I'm safer curled up in these blankets, with a heavy swaddled arm thrown over me, a rancid layering of old clothes and sweats hugging me close to him, pinning me to the mattress, and amid all this outrage and frustration, what I am doing is falling asleep, dozing off. Unless this is some badgerlike self-hypnosis to bury awareness.

I shouldn't have worried. From behind, insistent, his hand burrowed between my thighs, I clasp them closer, but there's no strength there, is he not even going to undress? why bother, it's hardly an aesthetic maneuver, just a simple direct, clumsy but effective route to satisfaction. His stubby cock between my thighs, hands grubbing down the waistband of my trousers, barely, rubbing, pushing into me, or near me, not threateningly hard or pathetically but dangerously flaccid, the danger his frustration will turn outward to violence, even then, part of me marvels at the lack of contact, the lack of any possible pleasure or communion, well, what I am I? a choirboy? or novice? what does he care, whether he can find one orifice, or two, or some cleft to rub off inside, I'm not concerned with anything, it's a shock to realize that I am indeed in my own bed, under my own blankets, and others, piled with overcoats, immobilized, until he spends himself on or around my crotch, and all hope lost, like a man who has climbed a hill, collapses exhausted, on me, in me, entwined, then dips back into his own depths, perhaps only a dream for him. Now could I do it, too late, there's a blade within reach, but what? All a matter of timing.

I can roll out of bed. Gather my clothing. But I forfeit my keys. You might think that revenge, immediate, in this hiatus, is the best tactic, but somewhere deep, I see the open window, the snowdrift beckons, and yes, I can force it a little wider. Am I to teach him a lesson?

He doesn't even move.
And out.

The fire escape dangles off single bolts. Ripped out to preserve the fortress, its impregnable entry. Trails downward but stops short, twenty feet above the lower rooftop. I have no rope.
The drop is too far. Sit there staring at the streets.

There's a bird above. Laughing. It would have to be a crow. Augury, it says. I look up.

The fire escape climbs uninterrupted to the building rooftop. Up is the new down.
I laugh back at the crow. A crowlaugh, just one birdbark. It cackles back, once. They can fly and they can walk. Smart. I get to the roof, best as I can. The crow, it, wheeling off, looking for someone else to laugh down on. Sister crow.

Up top, amid the ships' funnels and tubings of the air conditioning units and elevator winches, the escapes zed off to all sides. Many, yes, have been ripped out, but not all. In less then five minutes I am dropping onto the street, a thick drift breaking my short fall.
Then I walk.

It's the opposite of focus, in that I am incapable of dwelling on anything more demanding or less immediate than one foot in front of the other. Down the middle of the empty street, head down at the junction, going ever eastward, back into the lee with the sound of a thudding door, the flakes falling suddenly slowly, through liquid, soft, rather than horizontal, like glasspaper to the face.
But I still need to shuffle prophylactically into a doorway to catch my breath, to listen to my heart beat, lean back out of sight.

The music again, louder now, chimes from a happier time, then left to right, in a narrow gap, the truck glides by left to right, crisply embossing its tire tracks in the snow, and off.
I could catch up at a run, but I follow at a distance, at a walk. I cannot believe the driver does not see me, but then again, I do not see him. Or her. God help him, if he's a She. Or God help me.

So I follow, out along Canal, to the bridge, where the snow piles up, the abandoned cars solidify into an impenetrable barrier, and the truck slows to a stop.
Across the river, the glass cliffs and white stones of Brooklyn rise, heads lost in the clouds.

Clap.

So, one of the guys laughs and asks if I'd fancy an ice cream. In this weather?
Why not, everybody's got to make a living.
I guess so.

Which is why I allow myself to stop fretting about what may or may not be behind me, don't even take off my mittens to check on my fingers whether I have been asleep two days, two weeks, or two years, the faded rings under other faded rings, an unreadable dictionary of forgetting and edge up slowly to the pale blue Mister Softee van that's broadcasting its jolly jingle to the refreshment deprived sleepwalkers or the desert street.

A sure sign that summer is here.

Blizzard at my shoulder notwithstanding.

the one about the drones

THE SOUND has always been there, always, since birth, buzzing ceaselessly and causing the coal dust to shake off the windowsills and drop onto the formica tables. Buzz. Buzz. Dead flies of winter. Then suddenly, nothing. A long nothing. Monday nothing, Tuesday nothing, as the old song goes. Then only in dreams, or half dreams, surfacing awake from the depths, gasping for oxygen, if they still smoke oxygen. Mica for their cigarettes, flashing in the corners of bars, winking to invite you in, submerge you.

Waves from the sea, convoys passing overhead, or jet fighters scrambling low, then that shudder you feel in the belly, an uneasiness that you don't hear until it stops, and the silence lets the muscles relax. That sound.

It finally occurs to me that the world is not in fact winding down. It has already wound down.

Everyone has already left town, except those of us who can't afford to leave (I mean, literally do not have enough money to buy their way out) or those who haven't heard the news yet. Or that secret deluded group—the one I've fallen in with—who still cling to some remnant, figment, rumor of an old position, hard fought, tenaciously held, that has been long forgotten by everyone else. No-one even remembers to pull out the plug, switch off the lights on the way out. Amid all the chaos, the sudden emptiness, maintenance crews are not only still crawling over scaffolding, and refurbishing fake skylines; they are also still being paid, still paying their deductions and still drawing down pensions. Nothing to see here, they'd say, crouching on a girder jutting over Central Park, munching a sandwich and gazing off to Florida, vees of geese heading down, or coming back, who knows? At night no more lights to distract and disorient them. The mobile architecture of starlings. Hummingbirds and ravens.

The street-food is being laid out, if you want to struggle through the crowds, Alma serving her *pad thai,* her new-traditional sari falling off her shoulder in a bergamot diagonal, collarbone to hip, exposing her subtly tattooed left breast and, when she pivots, the similarly revealed smooth expanse of scapula. Probably why half the fauna flock here to watch Alma barely break sweat, but it's mesmerizing just to put those two words together like a pictogram: Alma, sweat. Gravity pulls down, sourdough rises. *Levure.* A loaf. *Chleb.*

Time has been slipping, like a baby's senses, fade in fade out and hazard the lapsed hours, days. The world turned dim, sound at the threshold of the audible, murmurings and mutterings subaqueous, come to think of it, the visible, too. Underexposed Polaroids, the faces knowing more, revealing less, passed. Oars dip under waves, their wake reaching a careless shore, weeks, months later, the geese still jockeying overhead, still or the cycle repeated, a year lost, they winter and return: geese migrate, but the Great Goose traces a lazy circle in time, year on year, eternal. The Earth in its orbit stuttering stroboscopic, not backward but not quite the full round ahead. It takes its toll. Nothing is sudden any longer. The sharpest changes import the weight of years. It has always been like this and the world is sinking. The crowd you idly stand with, thinned, aerated, bodies and faces scratched from the negative. The lively repartee become laconic. Audio drop out. Making us all mock-Lohengrinic on the sunset's shoreline. Not sunset, eclipse. The birds fallen mute, shadows vanished, footsteps halt. But the waves persist, lapping at an indecent rhythm, out of kilter. Perhaps the hearts slow or calm, monochrome. The breeze is still warm, but the hairs on your arm stand on end nevertheless.

The world seems so much thinner now; thinned out, the bright spots and point of contact extinguished, or separated by mountain ranges, oceans, division. What I mean is I am trying to measure the passage of time and there is no way I can. If not by holding memory against the tangible, what is lacking, what has gone? Suddenly different, suddenly less. I know, I said nothing sudden, but the realization, the revelation, keeps returning, so: sudden.

I have walked my trace over this city like a tattoo. Each street each way diversely. The glances, the odors, the sun pendant against every façade, shuffle the days, change routine to make the snipers' lives difficult. Which brings me back to. Rooftops, sights, that's not what it is, it's just what it reminds me of. The mountains are cut out of particle board into jagged *sierra* washed white and bleached, like some Wyoming billboard, backed with scaffold, footholds for the ganging crews. But the gangs have all gone home, skipped into entropy. I shade my eyes and gaze upward, out over Queens, a line of ice mountains horizon to horizon, sublimating mist. The city has gone, the electricity has gone, the gas has run out, the sea rises, the bergs ship ice-water, but you can walk across the sound at low tide, remarkably in all of this forgetting, these little bands of leather-skinned men are still up there fixing, protecting, wary, clocking in their nine-to-five, or the night shifts, still remarkably having numbers shifted in their favor and deductions made, stacked against time, drawing their pensions at thirty-five and retiring to the world that no longer exists in some other shadow flicker state. Bermuda, *¿Puede ser?* Or Rica Costa. Rico Puerto. Draw the line, lie back on the beach, let the tension seep out and dissolve in the sand. Stand, and fall, poleaxed. The blood got too thick. It's all down to water, never forget, the various configurations of its molecules we transport from ocean to desert to ocean.

Death is coming, in dreams, in the Vietnamese jungle; on an Istanbul hillside street; in a deep rock pool on a tide-locked beach, but I have always woken up. The ceiling fan beats. Neighbors. A chance to divine the weather by ear. Is it still night, or has the day begun? Hand on the bedside wall, cool, it thrums, the wall. Some truck or train or military convoy passing by, passing over, then the silence when it has gone, the shaking stopped. And another one. Stuck in the gray country. A train katang-danang, katang-danang, echoing some minor second. Dust caught in sunlight. Girders rivets.

Groaning corridors of groaning metal, expanding in the heat, contracting at night, a thousand times over, while the wind channels in makeshift alleyways, aeolian pipes at sub-sonic frequencies, shaking the crossbeams and loosening the bolts. A permanent not quite headache.

Staring at the empty cups, caught in early autumn sunlight through the incongruous lace curtains—thrift shop—in the former fisherman's house. Uphill in memory, it's such slow going, I dreamed of spider webs, and woke up wrestling with blankets, breathless, overheated.

Coming face to face with yourself is unnerving. Even an imprecise copy of oneself. A youthful folly, allowing my likeness to be used in an ad campaign, a guide to the dark side of town. A trickle of a little cash for a few weeks, then nothing, move onto the next gig. But what I didn't know, what none of us knew, was that the guides were never deleted, they just kept wandering around, looking for an ever-dwindling stream of unsuspecting clients, until the accounts timed out, or the last patchy networks failed.

But there we were. There he/me was. I am so glad I made me male. I think I'd have fainted if I'd bumped into a true waxwork doppelgänger. His eyes, friendly, scanned my face, as if unsure whether he remembered me or not. He's supposed to be a guide to the secrets of the city, but I am the one whose secrets he's revealing. Still faithfully in his holding position where he's supposed to pick up clients. So I ask him to take me somewhere I've never been.
Which he—it—I—J proceeds to do.

J down under the bridge that we still call the bridge though there's no water flowing beneath, not there, not now. J as I imagined him, remembered him. Everything I taught him, painstakingly input hour after hour, the bridge, too, half-remembered, reconstructed from memories, but looping out now over a canyon: an arched structure of some impressiveness nevertheless, and down the slope, that once-and-future riverbottom, there, dragged from the waves and wedged between rocks and the patched up *motogodilles* of the scavenger tribes. I could dilate on the significance or other of all their mock heraldic bandanas here, but later perhaps, if we are still speaking to each other. The ride out is all estival, whitecaps, the buzz of the outboard, the gentle vee of the wake, and the hypnotic sparkle of the sun motes, reflecting overbright, the temptation succumbed to of trailing the back of your hand in the water, surprisingly fresh, out of time like that, with a haze comforting you, as if this were some childhood memory, or if it is, then a layering of that memory over the present, how would you ever tell the difference, and if not past or present then how, with any certainty, not future? That's what they call immortality, I expect, the blissful ignorance of peril and its impossibility while you still dream, where waking up equals death, so dream on.

But I'm getting ahead of myself, as usual. Backtrack two days (though it was one unbroken stream of listless activity, in reality) to find me walking along Battery, over the mudflats and rubble to the Jersey ruins. That Lady's still holding her arm aloft, hailing a taxi in some parody of a welcome, but she's got her back turned, head full of thoughts elsewhere.

Wind in the hair again, and the motor's drone almost perky, cresting waves, into and out of mist banks, the sun slipping away, dim enough to gaze directly at, you could blot it out with a child's thumbnail, but it would still shine. Holding up my hand, stretching it out, I am that child again, and she is I, always that gentle hand stroking the star, and at night the moon, magical passes in the air to ward off the evil eye, then J cuts the motor, and everything falls silent. I am lying back over the edge of the boat, cool hand trailing. The cold cold water, the cool cool air. I think I am just relaxing but J tells me I am smiling; why would I smile at this reluctant half-assed enterprise, but he got me, so props to him, he's not the worst of the fishes in the sea, on the sea, and he's taking me 'home' as he puts it, which might have a sinister edge but where I am coming from that's all right, sinister is as sinister does and J isn't particularly sinister, I doubt he even notices how recklessly he advertises himself. Is advertised: Two slices of bravado with a side-order of chutzpah, to go, please. And let it be here noted that my idealized J would look askance, like some juvenile uncle, on the kids who surfed the subway cars when there were subway cars, and now here he is doing the same thing only in the water, on the water, under the water, as well as up up up higher than you can count, just for a look-see. Not my idea of avuncular advice, from a man who cannot swim.

So, where are we going and why?? That's two separate questions so it deserves two separate question marks. The answer is but one: the comm-tower. Last comm-tower. There used to be a few dozen, but the ones fixed on land have been longsince stripped of all useable metals and fittings. Though you would think that the sheer height and passive danger of the things would force people to stay off, but there's a roaring trade in crampons, hand chalk, a vivid chatter of climbing tips and horror stories, that time I almost… what happened to x, and so forth, cracked ribs, dislocated shoulders and chipped teeth all currency of the experienced hand, none of whom count more than twenty-five years on the fingers of their hands and feet. Not so. And I never knew why, but J would always grin and shake his head that way and say 'You'll see. You'll get it." A nicely programmed nuance, to add a little personal quirk. Have to hand it to them. And drifting out on the big swell, in the cooling mists, I got it. What's that beat? Some radio drifting off-station in the distance, or the song of a whale rising, tik-tok, tac-a-tac, then gone again. J clicking his fingernails? No, he's stock still, bar a gentle nodding of the head. I hear it too, and the lapping of the sea at the boat's keel. "There's still fish here." I'm nodding too. Maybe. There's also chunks of ice big enough to cave the boat in, capsize us and show the folly of learning to swim. Far better not anger the sea spirits and accept your fate instead of the futile undignified and disrespectful attempt to get back to land, to rescue. Just don't set off, if you feel like that. You don't even know which way to head. Rolling mists and walls of ice. Suddenly a clearing, and that sound again, but different now; you can hear, or imagine hearing, human voices under the steady din. A quiet din getting louder, sirens and chainsaws. Muffled explosions, sea thunder. Then calm. I'm awake now, for sure. J takes out his compass then starts the engine again, we putter off east, away from the city, careful but not hidden, and out into the ocean, while the city falls behind, listing slightly, howling and rumbling through the dawn.

The comm-tower is a good hour's trip, we only had to dodge a few sluggish smaller bergs, and once, only once, heard another boat in the distance. Patches of clear sea again, then back into fog until boom, right there in front of us, a massive shank of cable rears out of the water at forty-five degrees, heading up to lose itself in the newborn clouds. We are a mile away and still I see nothing. But I can hear it now, a low and surprisingly delicate sighing, a whistle or hum, layers rolling over layers, it comes it goes like the underfabric of silence.

M had her own theories about these nature noises, she said the wind is the sound the air makes when it comes, and what we hear are the moans and spasms under its caress.
The sea the same, only wilder. She used to talk pretty hot when she wanted.

But out here now, becalmed. The slow swell and lull of the water, innocent of waves, patterns of foam in abstraction, stretched and compressed, while the prow of the boat keeps ploughing open the waters, a gentle bifurcation that pulls us on, in. No way of distinguishing subject and ground, whether we are moving into it, or it is flowing past us like a river.

Out of the mist a sudden white wall, white and rust, sheer from the undulating surface. Which takes me back to

The warm bedclothes, why does sleeping in someone else's bed always feel so much warmer, more difficult to leave?? And the sun is on the other side, the day after full moon, and she is still asleep, the light laying over her shoulders, cheek buried in the pillow, I ask myself a non-question, isn't this enough, just this moment?? And back

The comm-tower goes up to infinity, straight up. I putter the boat around the base, seemingly uniform, until we see the rungs carved into the side, flaked off paint burning orange on the dirty white wall. J ties off the boat, or it magnetizes to the mooring, and we clamber up like the worst of sailors, no animal grace, just flailing to get high and dry. But at the top, maybe twenty rungs up, there isn't even a landing area, just a rim a few feet wide where the tower of the comm is more solidly built, a cylinder standing on a square. The column just shoots up, unceremonious, and here the rungs jut out like staples, a couple of feet apart. What now?

J says, "It's simple: you just climb up, and the higher you get, the more you can see." I am about to start but that's not part of his role. He's the guide, after all. "No, I'll go first. I won't fall, but you might, and you'd bring me down with you, so... hang on and if you need to rest.... don't." And off he goes.

The noises are louder now, coming from all around. I can hear the wind, but obviously, with the still drifts of sea-mist, there is no wind. You'd think we'd all have gotten used to that by now, the soundtrack that doesn't correspond to the image, the glitch in the edit that lets you know you're in one of the loops on the edge of the zone. But we haven't learned, we've just learned to navigate, and lean in to where the timelines synch up again. Then again, you could live your entire life outside of the zones and have the same glitches, and who blame for that? or the peasants in Guatemala who only ever see, at best, advertisements and government warnings, which to be honest you can do just as well or better with tv and billboards or a town cryer.

I mull these things over as I hit a climbing rhythm and get out of the fogs. The sun hits bright now, and

I have to squint. The rungs are very precisely spaced, though not built for my body size, so I am stretching just a little too much each time, and getting just a little less efficient. But I'm bearing up well. It's not that I don't look down—everyone tells me never look down, even on a fire escape or up a—I don't know what—a tree? nothing like this stupid pole sticking up out of the ocean and I am as high as any rooftop now, I can sense that, but there's no perspective, no reference point, just a clear down and a clear up, but I don't want to look up because that means leaning out and throwing my head back, and I do that once stupidly and have to hug onto the rungs, wrap my arms and legs around them in case I faint, could I even sleep like that? I don't think so, you'd just relax and untwine your limbs, slip off and maybe fall asleep going down. That would take thirty seconds, so you'd have the chance to wake up, too.

However high it feels, I am clearly still near the bottom of the mast, and this strange thing, around the corner comes a wind, out of nowhere. It wasn't there, then suddenly: cold fingers, a bloom on my cheek, the shoes start to feel slippery, the light sharper, the salt taste, and so I look up.

J is nowhere to be seen. Never has been, has he? And anyway, what does it matter? What possible thing could I ask him for? a hug? a hand up? I don't need to make those moves any more, just crawl vertical like a dog.

All the animals invaded my head, it wasn't dogs that were dangerous, they can be dogged after all, it was birds, promising some shortcut, it is all so simple when you're up there. The wind is your friend, except it isn't really, and humans and birds are off on separate branches of the tree, which as we all know you can't go back down, so it's onward and upward or not at all, like beauty, so here we are in the heart of the beautiful, and the wind isn't doing those romantic caressing things now, it's lost its temper and it's trying to rip you off and toss you like a ragdoll, whatever you may have heard to the contrary, mister wind is a mean bastard once he gets you on your own, and what are you doing up here anyway, girl? you knew what would happen, didn't you, so here I am, you can always turn back, but take the fast route, don't annoy me or disappoint me, or keep climbing. Where's J? Up top staring at the moon, no doubt. Did I tell you it is dark now? All dark now.

You construct people from your ideas of what they could be. And then set them off. But after that initialization, they go their own way. Even someone who comes from inside yourself goes their own way. You don't know them any more. And there you sit, above the clouds. Your fault.

I blink my eyes there and the world resets.

Back under the bridge, half a day earlier. The tide has turned, the waters risen, fogbanks flowed in from the sea, a deafening HUUUUUUNH-HUUUNH cutting through to tell us which way to go, to avoid, to flee to drift preciously inward, machetes held aloft, if we are tending to piracy. But the eyes are stuttering now. Perhaps the networks are down? Unreliable.

It makes you laugh. All those years of ads and exhortations to reach higher, be your best you, join the force, be soldier-strong, and in the end, the only channel that holds up is the Chinese one, down at street level or sub-street, none of those fancy towers or permanent 'premium' networks. It's golden dawn, it moves it shines, then cuts out crassly in the backstreets suddenly bustling again, matted with dirt and real stench, while the shiny ones look bewildered, no longer able to pick their way gracefully over the corpses, between the mounds of trash, in their white marble plazas. the ones lying low, finally overwhelmed by the compression of the world, while striding over their bodies, in machine tailored shoes and pristine slacks, eyes glued to the upper horizons, seeing who knows what epiphanies, the gilded youth stride on. Underfoot, it's all the eyes can do to swivel and follow their trails.

Nothing else works though, and unless you took up on those dimestore Mandarin classes (you didn't, did you?) so better get used to not understanding the signage, or the graffiti, only the numbers, still shrill, flashing in fluorescence: $19.99, and the bus company, still solid, loading up the laundry bags from the bang-bang ladies' water bottle sacks, those few that remain. You can't pick your way through that, and who knows, maybe it's inoffensive? just friendly electronic reminders to choose your hardware carefully, and a list of pleasant places you might like to flee to, or toward, depending on your current credit status. Like Iceland, for example, seen as that never quite caught on. Is that what J wanted to show me? The view from the mast? Something he's seen that I didn't teach him? It must be a broadcast mast, so high up here, you wouldn't need much of a signal, and there's no interference. But the vertigo is paralyzing. It looks a mile down. You can't look down. I can't.

I ask, are we a mile up? J just taps onto the rungs ascending, who knows, another mile higher. He's back in range.

"You can read, can't you?" yes, I can, if I shield my eyes like a self-blinkered horse, and what is a horse doing up here, so high? There's a small, hand-painted number behind the rung, it says: 1010. What's one-oh, one-oh?

Meters. That's three thousand, three hundred and thirteen feet. Only a little over half a mile. J can simplify things that way. Half a mile up, staring out, if he could see, at what would he see? But his hands, like some cartoon sea captain sweep the imaginary horizon, "Behold". So I behold. Against the sun, between the Battery and New Jersey - blocking the swamplands and refineries, the hundred floor tenements and the hectares of storage warehouses—snow-capped mountains reach up to the skies, jagged peaks catching the scatterings of sunlight, haloed, covering the waters of the bay, crystal clean, with a choppy golden luminance.

"Notice anything funny?"

Nothing was making me laugh.

"You don't laugh much any more, do you?" He has that knack.

Nothing makes me laugh.

He points at the Jersey Ice fields and gives me his Socratic spiel. I think he must've used to be a teacher or something, like, he'll never tell you something straight, he just points and wiggles his ears and waits for the penny to drop. It doesn't drop.

"Notice anything odd about the icebergs?" They look like they'd last a million years. A million years more. But I have to admit, they do look beautiful, in the light and all.

"You can only see the top ten percent of an iceberg,

right? Ninety percent underwater"
We all know that one, though in my old-school days, they used to say seven-eighths...
"...but they're sitting in a swamp"
That's where they towed them. They didn't just grow there like mushrooms.
"So, how'd they get thousand-foot icebergs into ten feet of mud?"
Never thought about it. Dig a trench? Chop the bottom off?
And he's right. They look like toy icebergs. Because they are toy icebergs.

J waves his fingers in front of my eyes, and the images shudder. Not just the fake icebergs, but the idealized sun, too. It's somewhere else, and casting longer shadows. I can see what's been happening across the river now, and it's not pretty, but hey, what you can't see can't hurt, right?
And now they've gone, even the Chinese channel isn't even bothered enough to big them up. The teeth are rotten, and most have been pulled. Grey walls, hollowed superstructures, papier-mâché and scaffolding

You have to turn your back to the sun, the real sun, and look off to sea. There's something out there, some dim shape, isn't there? Or am I imagining it? Perhaps a flake of snow got stuck on an eyelash, then melted, and then froze again.

It is just like J to abandon me, here, half a mile up a comm-tower, setting sun, otherwise romantic though I know I'm reading too much into it, J isn't romantic, can't be romantic, however hard I try to make him, or her, depending on his mood, or hers, or mine, in a shifting valley. So he just disappears.

Oh, I think, in the moment, he must have carried on climbing, but obviously no, he doesn't have the agency for that, if this is where he brought me to. But that's me all over, attributing agency willy-nilly, left and right. J, as usual, has simply divined my deepest secret wish, which isn't to say that I'd never expressed it before, sometime, in the recesses of memory, mine, his, whoever's. I'm rationalizing all this as rumor and gossip, when it's simply information exchange, I know. What I once glanced at that day, my frame of mind, the length of the pause, pause for thought, or other distraction? analyzed, weighed, numbered, stored... and so, my longing glances at iceberg after iceberg, my trips out to sea, my effable sadnesses and J's eagerness to please. Myself or some other. In some other's downtime, that must be it, I could never afford this much free rein, I must be surfing on somebody else's high-octane credit rating, up here, high and dry, beginning to freeze into the metalwork, what a curious way to die that would be, or else I could dive off and follow J, like some mythical sea eagle. How far down would I go? How deep the ocean? Or just stop on the surface, maybe there's rocks breaking right there, that would be a shock. So, no. No diving. No J. No point in going further up, as the mast grows slimmer and slimmer, ending for all I know in a needlepoint, to attract the lightning, or is it above the storms, like we would say a person is above their emotions? Like J, who nevertheless, in his intermittent presence, maintains a good humor, and maps onto my own kinda wry, begrudging irony. I always saw it that way. But who knows?

I climb down, have you ever tried to climb down a high mast, rung by rung, without looking below? And I'm obviously not the same body type as the guys who built this thing—listen to me, 'the guys', is if it was built by 'guys'... but somebody had once been up here, some body that could easier make the stretches between steps, backwards. You hit a rhythm, and I sing myself a little song, katang-danang, katang-danang, like the trains that used to run by our apartment all night, it was mostly the rails that made the noise though, not the trains, they just squealed and sparked, the rhythm was in the sleepers, and they pumped through the ground and made the building shake, everything and everyone hooked to the same beat, asleep or awake, synchronizing the two universes and fading into dawn, you'd never know what had driven past in the night, passed without stopping while I watched the light shadows on the ceiling, and the blur on the glass

danang-katang until I hit that bottom platform, an hour later, the boat still tethered, it would know the optimal way back all by itself, while I just lie, stunned, arms aching, looking up at the empty sky.

Perhaps I could find someone still in Chinatown? And so I miss what is surely there, winding in the alleys between ice, the snowmelt a trickle now, the steam lights throwing canyons into shadow. You can still hear the dull clatter of machinery, distant splashes, and changes in the tide, but all I can see are the backs of the flats, the wings of the facades, our working secret that it is all over, everything gone home, no holidays, done.

In Gowanus, the containers all ring empty, doors left open, swinging, or jammed shut to stop them banging in the wind, the gales. Up above the doppler screams and whines, jets take off and land, overladen land-trains, truck after truck, pull away in a shudder of diesel, the support columns of the thruway overpass visibly shaking, columns of fine powder dusting down. And what is up there, droning day long night long? It takes me a while to pluck up the courage to climb up and look. I think the comm tower must have cauterized my fear of heights (the one I never realized I had, even) and this is more akin to a child's puzzle, working my way up to the roadway box by box, overhanging girder by overhanging girder, until right at the peak, the safe haven of a maintenance ladder, protected by its own metal tube, popping me out on the edge of the road, deafening now, and

and nothing. Nothing on the road at all, deserted. Nothing moving, at least. A few abandoned burnt-out carcasses of cars and trucks, and here and there, strapped to the remaining lampposts, boxy loudspeakers, blaring out these rumbles, sounds you felt through your stomach, through your feet. It's what I'd heard up the tower, the high winds, the cables, the scraping of metal on metal, amplified here to what end? By whom? Song of the steel.

I'm past caring, to be honest, maybe it's something like J, but on a bigger scale. Something that was set up to help, but dug too deep into our real wishes, which are, it seems, no more than to lie down and be left alone, maybe a blanket to pull over our heads, in case it gets cold, because no-one wants to freeze to death, but to drift off warmly, why not?

I don't think that's what I have been thinking, in my heart of hearts. And then I got to thinking about M again, and what she might have been up to. I don't really know how to say that accurately, what I imagined she could have managed to be getting up to, had she been able to get up at all. So many unknowns.

In Chinatown, though I can't be sure about this, there are some people about. I mean, people. Not crowds or sidewalk fillers—actual people, who will need actual food and actual water and, these winter days, actual shelter, of nights. In one of those long thin stores, open all night, crowded with tins of cat-food and boxes of tea, I buy some chocolate from the storekeeper—a woman, I think—if it were a guide, it would smile—and the chocolate is real, even though the wrapper has been broken and the surface of the bar is mottled and pale, as if with leprosy.

I'm hoarding the last of my mica smokes in my pocket. It's been through the wars. It's a half-cigarette, really, I crimp it like a guilty teenager, feel it crackle between my fingers. Saving it for later. For a rainy night.

Along East Broadway, there's a double downpour now—the one in the net; and the real one. It makes distinguishing the passers-by easier—all of the extras are immediately furnished with any variety of luminous umbrellas, more advertising signage, while the real folks, caught out like the idiots we are, look like drowning rats in the downpour. Also, none of us are smiling. Surely some whizkid could have programmed that feature in: scowl occasionally. But these rats don't even frown, just scuttle closer to the walls and slip into doorways. The aesthetic rain is coming down in pleasing tropical sheets, feathering the skyscrapers, and stippling the roadway reflections, the designer palmtrees bending in the typhoon, but the real rain is icy, and you have to turn your back on it and hunch over, bunch your hood around your face (if you have one—a hood, I mean) and lurch round the next corner, eyes tight shut. Keep going.

I walk these streets, as I have done since before memory, always walking, one foot in front of the other, or skipping, floating on the thin air, hair bouncing on the nape of my neck, or yours; and you, you walk these same streets, too, but underground, burrowed inside, or lost somehow, and I was the fool who taught you that, how to work the angles, the angels you said, and now we can criss-cross the city and never meet again, because you are there, but I am here, perhaps twenty feet over your head, matching footsteps, or perhaps you hear my echo beneath, in the empty tunnel, and recognize my wings beat overhead, for a second, and then not at all.

In the village, I creep into the back blocks, hopping the low walls until I reach M's old building—our old building—and pull myself up onto the fire escape. I sit outside her window for an hour, plucking up the courage to break in. This is what mica is made for, and my last single ritual matchstalk.

Inside, I can see, my face pressed against the dirty glass, eyes shielded from the reflections behind me, that nothing has changed. Of course nothing has changed, how could it? The room is dark, only the half-light from the doorway onto the hall, and the monitors, all neatly stacked, with their pilot lights on, red dot lamps glowing, the shelving slicing up the space. And when M steps through, slowly, I do not see her at first, and she does not see me, she just stands, her head in shadow, her torso lit with blue light, her legs in shadow mid-thigh, unidentifiable, though I recognize her, the barrettes through her nipples, her breasts modest, perfect, as she turns and walks back into the dark hall.

The crackle of the burning, the flickers of vision, smoke slowly snaking through the traces of my red-lit reflection in the window, the rhythmic glow as I inhale, exhale, my face superimposed on the empty room. Then M walks back in again, comes to the window, stares out. How can she not see me? She looks through me, turns and walks back into the hallway. The sway of her hips; slight, boyish. I hold my hand against the window, trace the line of her body in the water droplets, as she turns and leaves the room, then I lift up the windowpane—it sticks at first, but then opens softly—so I can clamber inside and silently lower it closed behind me. Let the room engulf me. Suddenly the hiss of the rain cuts out: a new soundtrack. I sit down on the floor, crouched against the window behind stacks of electronics. All the cables behind the units tangle over me, and everything becomes warm hum. Mica this. Mica that. Like we used to do after long summer nights on the balcony. The weather's always there, whatever it may be.

Another loop of M comes back in, close enough to touch now, if I could.
But the time to touch her was then.

She stops in front of me, so close, her skin like hi-lacquer ceramic, runs in flat ridges, as if covered in rain, not seen through a window, but made of window. By the third time she leaves the room, I wonder if that's how she saw me, too, across the same courtyard, all those years ago. Each of us hiding out, staring across the same void from opposite angles, sundered angels, and call that love.

That's how I remember her. Of course, that's how she is remembered. And this is how I am remembered, on a fire escape in December, pulling the last drag of my last cigarette, gazing out of my own old window, across the lowest budget Chinese network,
as the icebergs melt
and the lights go off
And lie fallow and dark
And then click on again,
the whalesong drone of wind through cables doing its moorland thing regardless, unconcerned.

It's a beautiful world.

Photo: Renate Winter

About the Author

Russell Craig Richardson was born in the north of England and has lived in London, Paris, Valencia, and New York. His background is in film, television, translation, and education.

He has been telling stories all his life. This is his first book of fiction.

Acknowledgements

The author would like to thank everyone at Station Hill for making this book possible, especially Sherry Williams for her book design and layout work. Thanks also to Jacek Dziubiński and Jack Morelli for additional elements. Thanks for critical comment and encouragement to Robert Kelly and Charlotte Mandell; to Joel Newberger for his perceptive and sensitive edit work on the ms.

& to feu Pēteris Cedriņš for the kindest first words.

& thanks above all to Dorota, Dorota, Dorota, & Dorota